M

"Something wrong?" Spencer asked.

Biting her lip, Hannah turned the pail over. Bold red letters spelled out the word *English*. A red slash cut across the entire bottom of the pail, as if to say, *No English Allowed*.

Her knees grew weak. Suddenly the heavy cotton of her Amish dress clung to her neck, making her hot, strangling her. She pushed past Spencer and returned to the first pail and found the same thing.

"Look," she said, handing him the bucket. "The person who slashed my tires was busy last night."

Spencer's brow furrowed as he glanced down at the bucket.

"You have to find my sister's husband. If it's he who's doing this," she quickly added.

"We're doing everything we can to find him," Spencer said, his gaze intent on her. "To get answers."

The thought of spending another long, restless night in this house...

"To answer your earlier question, I won't leave, won't abandon my nieces. Because—" she swiped the bucket out of his hand "—that's exactly what her killer wants me to do."

Alison Stone lives with her husband of more than twenty years and their four children in western New York. Besides writing, Alison keeps busy volunteering at her children's schools, driving her girls to dance and watching her boys race motocross. Alison loves to hear from her readers at Alison@AlisonStone.com. For more information please visit her website, alisonstone.com. She's also chatty on Twitter, @Alison_Stone. Find her on Facebook at facebook.com/AlisonStoneAuthor.

Books by Alison Stone

Love Inspired Suspense

Plain Pursuit
Critical Diagnosis
Silver Lake Secrets
Plain Peril

Visit the Author Profile page at Harlequin.com.

PLAIN PERIL

ALISON STONE

HARLEQUIN® LOVE INSPIRED® SUSPENSE

 LOVE INSPIRED BOOKS

Recycling programs for this product may not exist in your area.

ISBN-13: 978-0-373-67662-0

Plain Peril

And we know that God causes everything to work together for the good of those who love God and are called according to his purpose for them.
–Romans 8:28

To my big sister, Lisa, whose gift was reminding all of us
to *Live, Love, Laugh.*

To Scott, Scotty, Alex, Kelsey and Leah.
Love you guys, always and forever.

ONE

The long shadows from the branches clacking against the bedroom window stretched across the two small lumps in the queen-size bed. Hannah tucked the hand-stitched quilt—the one her grandmother had made—under her six-year-old niece Emma's chin and smiled. A pathetic smile. The poor child stared back, a cross between grief and contempt on her precious little face. On the other half of the bed, Sarah, Emma's nine-year-old sister, had already lost the battle against the flood of tears, and sleep had taken her. Merciful sleep.

Hannah blinked her gritty eyes a few times and drew in a deep breath, praying for wisdom.

"I want *Mem*." The plea in Emma's tiny voice tore at Hannah's heart.

I want your mem, too. But Hannah kept those words locked in her heart along with her conflicting emotions. She kissed her niece's cool forehead. "Sleep, little one. I'll be here in the morning."

Emma pursed her lips, unimpressed with the promise of another day with Aunt Hannah.

How many more mornings could Hannah maintain this routine? She had already been here for three days, and she only had two weeks before she had to return to her job as a bank teller in Buffalo. She tried to quiet her mind and prayed the young girls' father would return home soon. Everyone had anticipated that her sister's husband, John, would returned for his wife's funeral.

Everyone was wrong.

Hannah's chest tightened. The circumstances surrounding John Lapp's disappearance were sketchy at best. Would leaving these two sweet girls with the father who had abandoned them at the most critical time in their lives be the best option—even if he did return?

A little voice told Hannah John was not going to return.

Emma crinkled her nose at Hannah. The familiarity of the gesture took Hannah's breath away. How many times had she seen Ruth make that same face when she was a little girl? *Poor Ruthie.* Hannah smoothed her niece's hair, and the child jerked away.

Hannah's heart broke a little bit more.

"*Guten nacht*, Emma. I love you." Hannah took a step toward the door. Every inch of her ached for her precious nieces who had lost their mother in a horrible farming accident, after which their father had apparently run off in grief upon finding her body partially buried in the grain silo.

She shook her head, trying to dismiss the horrific image. She ran her hand along the smooth railing on the stairs. The swooshing of her long dress brushing against her legs felt strange yet familiar. She slowed at the bottom of the stairs, allowing her eyes to adjust to the gathering darkness. She hadn't bothered to turn on the gas-powered lights before she had headed upstairs to tuck the children into bed.

Now she didn't mind lingering with the long shadows. It suited her mood. She wondered fleetingly what time it was, then realized it didn't matter. The children and the chores on the farm dictated her day. Not a clock.

Through the front window, she noticed the sun low on the horizon. Soon the entire house would be cast in darkness. Then she'd be left with nothing but her thoughts because sleep didn't come for the guilt ridden. A chill skittered up her spine, and her neck and shoulders ached from exhaustion. She dreaded the long night in her childhood home in the middle of nowhere.

She wished she had something mindless to occupy her time, like TV or her iPad, two things she had reluctantly given up when she stepped foot into her sister's Amish home.

Her dead sister's home.

Her eyes drifted to the far wall in the room, an

empty spot where her sister's simple pine casket had held her body as friends and neighbors came to give their final respects. She closed her eyes and felt the familiar tingling, the promise of more tears. How could it be that her younger sister was dead? She sighed heavily. Hannah had abandoned her Amish ways, but she hadn't abandoned her faith. She'd get through this. For the sake of her nieces, she had to.

Hannah found herself in the kitchen putting on the teakettle. She stared over the yard and daydreamed about the days she and her sister—two years younger—had run in and out of their mother's fresh sheets hanging on the line. The scent of clean laundry and newly cut hay. Not a care in the world.

A nostalgic unease wormed its way into her memory. No cares as long as *Dat* was busy working on the farm because as soon as his chores were done, he'd find a reason to scold Hannah while allowing Ruthie to play undisturbed with her dolls.

Hannah never understood the favoritism. Now, more than a decade after she had slipped away from Apple Creek in the middle of the night, she felt the emptiness. An emptiness that had kept her away.

Until now.

A knocking at the door startled Hannah. She turned off the gas stove. Her pulse whooshed in her ears as her long gown whooshed around her calves. Had her sister's husband, John, finally returned?

Doubt whispered across her brain. Why would he knock on the door of his own home?

Why would he abandon his daughters after their mother's tragic death? John was obviously not well.

She drew in a deep breath and reached for the door handle. What could she possibly say to him? Could she muster the compassion her brother-in-law needed? She feared she'd be unable to hold back the torrent of angry words criticizing him for not manning up when it came to his bereaved children. She yanked open the door, praying for the former. The greeting froze on her lips.

"Miss Wittmer, I'm sorry to bother you so late. I'm Sheriff Spencer Maxwell. We met earlier today."

Alarm sent goose bumps racing across her skin.

"Yes, Officer?" Self-consciously, Hannah smoothed her apron and skirt, an outfit she wore out of deference to her grieving mother. Hannah's English wardrobe would have been an in-your-face reminder that her mother had lost not one, but two daughters. The handsome sheriff had paid his respects at the funeral earlier today in the barn. He was one of only a few outsiders to mingle among the hundreds of Amish. That's the reason she noticed him, or so she told herself.

The sheriff removed his hat and pressed it to his chest revealing short-cropped hair and kind eyes. "I almost didn't stop when I noticed the lights weren't on, but I took a chance."

Something in his tone made the fine hairs on the back of her neck stand on edge. "It sounds important." She didn't invite him in, fearing the neighbors would question why a single Amish woman—she referred to herself as Amish in the loosest of terms—had invited a man into her home. Part of her wondered why she cared. "Do you have news regarding my brother-in-law?"

"No, I'm sorry. I don't." His even tone gave nothing away. "But I do have something important to discuss."

Hannah listened for any sounds from the bedrooms. It was quiet save for the chirping of the crickets floating in through the open windows on the warm summer evening. Hannah hoped Emma had finally drifted to sleep. Hannah stepped onto the porch, pulling the door closed behind her. "Let's talk out here."

Hannah sat on one of the rockers, fearing her legs wouldn't hold her upright. She was still struggling to get over the news that her sister had died. Her twenty-seven-year-old sister.

Sheriff Maxwell walked the length of the porch slowly then turned around and stopped in front of her. He leaned back on the porch railing. He seemed to be collecting his thoughts, but his hesitation made her feel suspicious, like when a man wandered into her bank with sunglasses and a baseball cap tugged low over his eyes. "Please sit,

Officer Maxwell. You're driving me crazy and if you don't sit, I'm going to lose it."

The sheriff angled his head and studied her for a minute. She knew the look. Something wasn't adding up in his head. She had seen it many times, mainly in Buffalo. It was the double take of a bank patron when the word *yah* slipped from her lips. Or the pestering of her coworkers who couldn't understand why she didn't join them for happy hour. Or her roommates, who playfully mocked her unassuming wardrobe.

Now her English vocabulary was invading her Amish ruse.

The sheriff lowered himself into the chair next to hers and ran his hand along the smooth wood of the arm. "You seem different than the other Amish women I've met."

And there it was.

Hannah flattened her hand against her prayer covering and forced a smile. "Is my bonnet on crooked?" After burying her sister and suffering withering looks from her former Amish neighbors and so-called friends, she was in no mood to be scrutinized by the sheriff, too.

The setting sun reflected in his brown eyes, and his brows shifted, as if he were adjusting his line of thinking. Regret at her snippy comment teased her insides, but not enough to apologize.

"I didn't mean to pry." He tapped his fingers on the arm of the chair. "I have some difficult news."

Hannah hiked her chin and tried to ignore her racing heart. "At this point, I'm numb to bad news."

"You've had a rough time of it." Sheriff Maxwell's Adam's apple moved in his throat, and his hesitation made her panic swell, forcing all the air from her lungs. She wasn't as numb as she claimed to be. He shifted toward the edge of the rocker and looked like he wanted to reach out and take her hand, but thought better of it.

Hannah sent up a silent prayer.

Dear Lord, please be merciful and let me handle whatever it is this man has come here to say.

"Yesterday, I drove out to Bishop Lapp's farm."

"John's father." The elder Lapp had to be escorted by the arm into the barn for his daughter-in-law's funeral. His stooped posture radiated his grief. The bishop had only a few terse words for Hannah. It didn't come as a surprise, considering the bishop's loss and Hannah's non-grata status in the community.

"The bishop's other son, Lester, dismissed me without hearing what I had to say." The sheriff stared toward his vehicle parked on the side of the road; its presence no doubt had the neighbors' tongues wagging. Wireless technology had nothing on the old-fashioned rumor mill in Apple Creek.

"Bishop Lapp must be having a difficult time." Hannah said the first polite thing that popped into her head. She had no firsthand knowledge on how he was doing. Since Hannah had never been baptized, she wasn't officially shunned, but the bishop was determined to freeze her out all the same.

"I understand, but I need to talk to him about his son, John."

"I'll be of no help there."

"It's important you know where the investigation is headed, especially since you're staying in John Lapp's house."

A hot flush swept over her body. "This was my family's home before John moved in with my sister."

"I understand." Spencer sounded contrite, but determined.

She tugged on the folds of her skirt to allow the fresh evening air to cool her shins and bare feet. "You're investigating my sister's accident?"

"Yes. It's customary for the medical examiner to be called out after a death like this. Law enforcement needs to make sure there was no foul play involved."

Apprehension prickled Hannah's scalp. She winced and scratched her hair through the fabric of the cap. Her tight bun was giving her a headache. "My sister's death was an accident. A tragic farming accident." That's what everyone had repeated over and over as they paid their final respects and then again when they delivered casserole dishes with wordy instructions on how to warm them up.

Such a shame. A tragic farming accident. And those poor girls, to lose their mother...

They'd shake their covered heads then bustle into the kitchen and make tsking sounds at her nieces, who sat cross-legged on the floor, stacking blocks.

What was left unsaid, but blatantly obvious in their Amish faces, was that if John had been a better husband, Ruthie wouldn't have been left with the brunt of the chores while her husband fraternized and schemed. What exactly he had been scheming, Hannah's mother wouldn't tell her.

Apparently, John Lapp hadn't entirely shed his youthful, rebellious ways.

This wasn't news to Hannah.

Sheriff Maxwell stood and faced her. The setting sun behind him cast his face in shadows. Tension hung heavy in the air. "There's no easy way to say this." The shaky quality of his voice made icy dread pool in her stomach.

"Tell me." She wrapped her fingers around the arms of the chair and squeezed.

"Before your sister ended up in the silo, she was already dead."

Miss Wittmer slumped in the wood rocker. Spencer's first instinct was to reach out, grab her, but she clutched the arms of the chair and stiffened her back, as if determined to be strong, regardless of the devastating news. The color draining from her face told a different story.

She drew in a deep breath. "I…I don't understand." The Amish woman rose and stood next to him. A thin strand of brown hair poked out from underneath her bonnet. She turned to face him, her eyes shiny with unshed tears. "Are you telling me my sister was murdered?" Her tone was shaky, brittle.

"I'm afraid so." Spencer let his hand hover near her elbow, ready to grab her if she should faint. She stood absolutely still, and he thought he heard Miss Wittmer's gasp above the incessant chirping of the crickets. As a cop originally from the inner city, he still hadn't gotten used to the racket nature created.

She shook her head briskly, as if trying to shake away the image, or perhaps his words. "My sister was murdered." It was no longer a question.

This time there was no mistaking her gasp. Spencer clutched her elbow. She crumbled to her knees, her thin frame swallowed in a pool of black material. She bowed her head. Spencer had seen loud grief—the wail of a mother who had lost her child in a drive-by shooting. He had never seen such a quiet, heartbreaking display. He didn't know how to react, and he didn't know which was worse.

Spencer crouched next to the woman and held her arm. "Let me help you up. I can get you some water. A cold washcloth. Something."

"Who did this?" Her words came out, barely a whisper.

"We're investigating."

The woman brushed his hand away and grabbed the railing and pulled herself to her feet, a mix of embarrassment and anger lacing her tone. "Ruthie told me she was afraid."

Spencer's pulse ratcheted up a notch.

Miss Wittmer yanked off her bonnet. The moon rising above the trees lit on the golden strands of her dark hair. If she weren't an Amish woman, he would have thought she had highlighted her hair. She smoothed a hand over the few loose strands that had sprung free from the bun at the nape of her neck.

She sat, resigned. "She told me she feared too many things were changing." She leaned back and wrapped her fingers around the arms of the chair. "My sister and I hadn't seen each other for over a decade, then about five months ago, she called me. She wanted to see me."

Spencer rubbed his jaw. "I guess it's my turn to be confused. She called you?"

Miss Wittmer looked up at him, a battle waging behind her watchful eyes. "John had a phone installed in the barn." She shrugged. "Claimed he needed it for work."

"And you have a phone, too?"

"I'm not Amish."

Spencer bit back a comment.

"I left Apple Creek and the Amish community eleven years ago." Miss Wittmer dragged her lower lip through her teeth. "It—" she lifted her palms "—this life wasn't for me. Once I left, my father refused to allow me to visit."

"You were shunned." Spencer had been sheriff of Apple Creek for only a year, but he was slowly learning the ways of the Amish.

She shook her head. "I was never baptized, so technically, there was no reason to shun me. But my father was a controlling man. He was part of the reason I left. I felt suffocated. And I suppose there was always the fear that if I came back home for a visit and talked about my wonderful, worldly life, who's to say my sister wouldn't want to leave with me." Heavy shadows masked her expression, but Spencer thought he detected an eye roll when she referred to herself as *worldly*.

"The clothes." He gestured to her long gown, her apron, the bonnet in her hand.

"It's easier this way. I wanted to make sure I respected both my sister and my mother." She grabbed a fistful of material by her thigh and fluttered her skirt. "This is my sister's." Her words came out droll, sad, lifeless as if to say, "She won't be needing it anymore."

A thought nagged at Spencer, and he didn't know how to broach it. He decided to be direct. "If you were estranged from your family, why did they contact you when your sister died?"

A mirthless laugh escaped her lips. "My mother, who wouldn't dare use the phone herself, sent word through a neighbor. I'm her only surviving child. My father's gone. Now my sister's gone." She sighed heavily. "And someone needs to take care

of the children…until John returns." The tone of
the last three words convinced him she understood
John was unlikely to care for his children when and
if he did return.

"No other family can care for the children?"

"John's family is busy searching for their son
and brother. They believe he ran off in grief after
finding Ruthie in the silo. Perhaps blaming himself.
His new job has taken him away from the farm."
She rocked slowly in the chair. "My mother is not
as strong as she used to be. She'd never be able
to manage two young girls." She stopped rocking.
"I'm worried about my *mem*. The news Ruthie was
murdered will devastate her all over again."

"I'll do my best to find whoever did this." He
studied Miss Wittmer's face to see if she had the
same suspicions he had. "Why was Ruthie worried
things were changing?"

"Ruth embraced the Amish way. When we were
kids, she spoke of raising her family here. She was
doing that. She had two beautiful daughters. By all
outward appearances, she had what any humble
Amish girl could want."

"What about her husband? Was her husband a
good guy?" John Lapp had come under his radar
once or twice, which definitely wasn't a good thing.

"I didn't know John. He returned to Apple Creek
shortly before I left. He was one of a group of young
men who had left the area to work on a ranch out
West. A handful of them returned and embraced

the Amish way and were baptized and married."
She drew in a deep breath and let it out slowly. "It
was the talk of the community. The families considered themselves blessed because their wayward
sons had returned."

"The prodigal sons." Spencer referred to the
parable he remembered from his childhood days
in Sunday school. Before he realized God didn't
bless all His children, especially poor ones born
into bad neighborhoods where guns and hanging
out on street corners crowded out God and Sunday
church services.

"Something like that." Miss Wittmer seemed unimpressed. "But no one killed a calf in celebration
of their return. Everyone went about their business.
If you haven't noticed, *we* are a humble people."
She wiggled her bare toes.

"Do you know if your sister and John had a good
marriage?"

"When we got together for the first time five
months ago—my sister drove the wagon to the Mc-
Donald's in the next town—she said she was worried that John didn't seem content. She feared he
might leave her and the girls. John had given up
farming for the most part and had taken a job making fancy swing sets."

Spencer pointed toward the road with his thumb
and squinted. "The place down the road? A lot of
Amish men are employed there." The Amish were

notorious for being hardworking, skilled laborers. No shame in that.

"That was the first change. John also spent more time with the men whom he had left with years earlier."

"Do you know these men?" Rumors reached the station that there had been some discord within the Amish community. When he tried to investigate, the alleged victims, men who had their beards cut in the middle of the night, refused to talk to him. Even Ruth Lapp had sent him away when he had come to this very farm to question her about her husband's possible involvement. But there was no mistaking the fear in her eyes. Ruth Lapp was afraid of something.

Miss Wittmer got a distant look in her eyes, as if she were replaying a memory. "Ruth never gave me the names of the men John was hanging out with. I've been gone a long time. The names may not have meant much to me." She ran her pinched fingers down the long tie on the bonnet in her hand. "There was something I found strange. My sister made what I thought was a passing comment about taking care of her girls. I laughed at her." Regret and grief flashed in her eyes. She sniffed. "When I realized she wasn't joking, I assured her she was doing a great job as a mom but if the time ever came, I'd make sure Emma and Sarah were well taken care of."

Her gaze drifted up to meet his. "Do you think she knew something was going to happen to her?"

The memory of Ruth Lapp shooing him off the farm so that her husband wouldn't find him here had haunted him from the moment he heard of her untimely death.

"Your sister seemed afraid, but she wouldn't open up to me."

Miss Wittmer's head shot up. "Why didn't you do something. Protect her?"

Spencer shoved his shoulders back despite the punch to his gut. "She assured me everything was fine. She told me to go, reminding me that the Amish and law enforcement have a tenuous relationship at best. There wasn't much more I could do if Ruth didn't talk to me."

Miss Wittmer bowed her head, and her shoulders sagged. "I was helpless when it came to my sister, too. I had no right to snap at you." Clasping her hands in her lap, as if she were bracing for something, she asked, "How do you know my sister's death wasn't an accident?"

"The county medical examiner didn't find any corn in her mouth or nose. If your sister had suffocated in the silo, she would have inhaled the corn."

Miss Wittmer closed her eyes. "He killed her, didn't he? John Lapp killed my sister."

Spencer cleared his throat. "We're still investigating. The Lapp family has been unwilling to talk to me. I'll give them a day or two to reconsider."

Miss Wittmer rubbed her arms, despite the mild evening. Her bonnet had been abandoned on her lap. "How cooperative do you think they're going to be when you accuse their son of killing my sister?"

"It's part of my job."

"I don't envy you." She planted her elbow on the arm of her chair and rested her chin in her palm. "I don't envy either of us."

TWO

Hannah tossed and turned on a small cot in the first-floor bedroom of her childhood home, now her sister's home. Even the white noise of the crickets couldn't lull her to sleep, not after the news she had received from Sheriff Maxwell. He had left her with a warning to be careful, his cell phone number and a promise to have his officers patrol her property.

Small consolation in the dead of night in the middle of nowhere.

Not even knowing that her mother slept nearby in the adjacent *dawdy haus* could calm her nerves.

The small bedroom grew stifling, yet she still couldn't bring herself to move to her sister's more spacious bedroom upstairs. Hannah slipped out of bed and slid the window open. She dismissed her silly fears that someone would climb through her window because if someone really wanted to get in, all they had to do was stroll through the front door. It didn't have a lock.

Hannah flopped down on the cot and sighed. She pulled the sheet up to her chin and stared toward the open bedroom door, imagining the shapes morphing into an intruder, namely John. She was driving herself crazy. Her nerves felt like they were jacked on too much caffeine.

Had John really killed her sister? The sheriff had warned her they didn't have enough evidence to prove John had been involved. But still...

Hannah struggled to quiet her mind with prayer and the hope of sleep. The chirping crickets filled her ears, and she realized the noise could also mask footsteps on creaking floorboards.

Tingles of dread crept up her spine.

"You're being silly. You lived in the city and never were this afraid," she whispered into the night.

You never tried to fall asleep with the knowledge your sister had been murdered.

Sitting up, she leaned against the wall and tipped her head back. The piece of snitz pie she had eaten before bed didn't seem like such a good idea. She was making herself sick with anxiety.

Just when her rational side had talked her irrational side out of a full-blown panic attack, the blaring of a car alarm sliced through the cacophony of chirping. Hannah bolted upright and snapped her attention toward the window. Her car was parked behind the barn and covered with a tarp.

She pressed a hand to her thumping chest and drew in deep breaths.

The alarm will turn off by itself. It will turn off by itself.

How many times had a car alarm gone off in the city? Especially on her street filled with college students and their varying schedules. Car alarms were sensitive. An animal probably scampered across the tarp. Or a tree branch dropped on it. Or…or…

No, it did not mean someone was out there waiting for her. Her apprehension grew with the strident pulsing of the alarm. She drew in another deep breath through her nose and released it.

Hannah threw back the sheet and climbed out of bed. She pushed back her shoulders. *I'm being ridiculous.*

She grabbed her cell phone from the end table and dialed six digits of Sheriff Maxwell's phone number, ready to press the seventh digit if needed. She grabbed a flashlight and her car keys from the kitchen on her way out the door. She stopped long enough to stuff her feet into boots.

Her focus tunneled. She made a direct path to her car, tucked neatly between the barn and a dense crop of trees. Striding across the yard, she rolled her ankle in a rut. "Whose great idea was it to park my car way out here? Oh yeah, mine," she muttered. Hannah was doing everything possible to comfort her mother, even if it meant hiding everything that made her an outsider.

The alarm came at Hannah in varying waves of ear-piercing obnoxiousness. Wincing, she lifted her key fob and aimed it in the general direction of the car and hit the alarm button. The sudden silence deafened her. Even the crickets were mute. She glanced back toward her mother's dark residence. Apparently, the noise hadn't disturbed her.

Hannah debated about returning to the house, but decided to quickly check on her car. She rounded the corner of the barn, and the beam of a flashlight blinded her. Her heart leaped in her chest, and she turned to run.

"Wait." A deep, commanding voice vibrated through her.

Hannah didn't wait. She had to put distance between herself and the man trespassing on the farm. She was out here alone. She had to protect the girls. She bolted toward the house, calculating how she'd reach the girls' room and wedge something against the door.

She stumbled in a wagon wheel rut and pitched forward. Crying out in panic, she braced herself. Pain shot up the heels of her hands as they met the earth. Her knees slammed down hard on the packed dirt.

"Miss Wittmer, it's Sheriff Maxwell."

On all fours, Hannah dropped her head in relief. She pushed to her feet and brushed the dirt from her palms and her pj's. She spun around. "What are you doing? You scared me to death."

"What are *you* doing out here? You shouldn't be wandering alone outside." The sheriff arched the beam of the flashlight across her dirty pj bottoms and her University at Buffalo T-shirt, complete with boots she obviously should have laced up.

"Don't answer my question with a question." Hannah crossed her arms and huffed. She had a tad more confidence in her English pj's than she had wearing her sister's Amish dress. No one expected her to fake Amish while she slept, did they?

"I was patrolling the area and heard the alarm." Sheriff Maxwell flicked his flashlight toward her vehicle. "Yours?"

She didn't bother to answer the obvious. He tossed back the tarp, revealing her three-year-old Chevy Malibu. "Someone slashed your tires."

Hannah plowed a hand through her hair, and a mix of annoyance, resignation and fear wound their way up her spine. "Did you see anyone?"

The sheriff shook his head. "I'm afraid not."

She glared at him skeptically. "Why are you lurking around here?"

"I'm not lurking. I'm doing my job." An annoyingly coy smile played on his lips.

"If you were doing your job—" she held out her hand toward her car, the one with twenty-seven remaining car payments "—then this would have never happened."

"Fair enough." His smooth voice rolled over her.

"But doesn't it make you feel better to know I'm not far away if you need me?"

Hannah smoothed the tarp back over her car. "Let's be clear about something. I don't need anyone."

He seemed to give her a once-over. "That's debatable."

Hannah swept her hair into a ponytail and fastened it with a rubber band from her wrist. "Fair enough." She repeated his words. "I am glad you're here. Find out who did this. But make sure you're not lurking around too much. I don't want the neighbors talking. They already give me enough grief."

Hannah spun around—her snippiness fueled more from her adrenaline-soaked nerves than from anger—and marched up to the house, keenly aware that Sheriff Maxwell was watching her.

The next morning, Hannah slipped into her sister's black Amish dress, an outward sign she was grieving. She peeked in on her sleeping nieces and decided to check on *Mem*. Through the screen door of the adjacent *dawdy haus*, Hannah saw her mother sitting at the kitchen table with a cup of coffee. When Hannah knocked, her mother pushed back from the worn pine table slowly. Hannah couldn't be sure, but she thought she saw her mother wince.

"Are you okay?" The screen door squeaked, and Hannah stepped into the small space. Memories crowded in on her. Hannah had spent long hours here visiting her own grandmother. Her mammy was the one person who loved her unconditionally. When Mammy died shortly before Hannah turned sixteen, Hannah had found herself rudderless between an overdemanding father and a too-passive mother.

"Tired is all." Her mother waved away her daughter's concerns. "Would you like coffee?" She took a step toward the stove.

"No, I can't stay long. I want to make sure I'm in the house when Emma and Sarah wake up."

Her mother shook her head in disbelief. She did that a lot since Ruthie died.

"Did you hear the commotion outside last night?"

Her mother paused. "Commotion?"

"My car alarm went off." She omitted the part about the slashed tires. She hated to add to her mother's grief.

"Neh." Her mouth pursed her lips. "My hearing is *neh gut."*

Hannah leaned against the counter and watched her mother slowly sit back down. Her mother took a sip of coffee then touched her head. "Your *kapp."*

Hannah tugged on her apron with both hands. "But I'm wearing a dress."

Her mother looked down without saying anything, renewed disappointment etched in her pale features. An expression Hannah had seen many times. An expression that had both frustrated and

confused Hannah as a teenager. Why didn't her
mother say what she meant?

"*Mem*, I came back for Sarah and Emma…and
you." Hannah pulled out the chair across from her
mother and sat. She angled her head to see into
her mother's eyes. "I don't know what my future
holds."

Her mother lifted her brows. "Your sister said
you were coming home." Her hopeful tone broke
Hannah's heart.

Hannah dipped her chin, surprise making her
momentarily speechless. "Ruthie told you about
our visits?" Ruthie had sworn her to secrecy.

Her mother nodded. *"Yah."* She fingered the
handle of the coffee mug. "Are you ready to be baptized Amish? Find a nice Amish boy and marry?
Maybe next year you can prepare—"

"No." The single word came out sharp, angry.
Hannah flattened her palms on the table and drew
in a calming breath and said more softly, "Not yet,
Mem. Not yet." Hannah scratched her forehead.
"I'll admit, I wasn't happy in Buffalo." She was
lonely and didn't enjoy her job, but she hadn't decided to return to the Amish way of life. Not permanently anyway. She was toying with the idea.
Searching for happiness. Wondering out loud to her
sister if she had been naive in her decision to leave
the Amish community in the first place.

Perhaps saying as much to please her sister.

Or perhaps, in a way, dissuading her sister from

making any big decisions that would alter her life irrevocably. As Hannah's decision had forever changed her life.

Hannah covered her mother's hand. "I'm here for the short-term until I know the girls are okay. Please, don't get your hopes up about me returning for good."

Disappointment creased the corners of the older woman's sad eyes. "I thought with *Dat* gone…"

Although the rift between Hannah and her father was apparent to anyone with eyes, it pained her to hear her mother talk about it.

"*Mem*, please, let's talk about this another time. We're all trying to come to terms with Ruthie."

"*Gott* has a plan."

Hannah's body tensed. "I wish God's plan was to leave Ruthie here on earth with us. With her daughters."

Her mother's lips quivered. "Life is hard. You have to make decisions that are *gut* for the family. You can't be selfish."

The sting of her mother's comments wounded her. Had Hannah been selfish?

"One day at a time, okay?" Hannah hated throwing out a silly platitude, but she wasn't ready to make life-altering decisions right now.

Will I ever be ready?

Hannah didn't want to discuss Ruthie's husband, but it couldn't be avoided. Not with John running around out there, somewhere. "Did Ruth ever say anything negative to you about John?"

Her mother's eyes flashed momentarily dark. *"Neh."* She shook her head vehemently. "I don't know how things work in the English world, but a woman does not speak ill of her husband. And if she does, she's just being gossipy."

"I'm not gossiping." She placed her elbow on the table and rested her chin on the heel of her hand. "Was John ever mean to Ruth?"

"John Lapp is the bishop's son." Agitation shook her mother's hands, and she refused to meet Hannah's gaze.

"John left Apple Creek when he was a teenager. He was gone for a long time. Maybe he wasn't the son the bishop had raised."

Her mother lifted her chin. "John came back. Was baptized. Married. It was *gut*." Which was more than Hannah had done. The accusation in her mother's eyes made Hannah's cheeks fiery. Couldn't her mother see she was doing everything she could? Everything short of promising to be baptized Amish.

"You like John Lapp?"

"Your sister and her husband took care of me. I am grateful to them."

Unease settled in Hannah's belly. Learning Ruthie was murdered would kill her mother. Hannah pushed away from the table. The whole truth would wait for another day.

Hannah brushed a kiss across her mother's soft cheek. Her mother pulled back and widened her eyes, startled by the display of affection. Hannah started to leave but turned back one last time. Her mother was holding her fingertips to her cheek, where Hannah had kissed her.

"Burning the midnight oil, huh?" Mrs. Greene, Spencer's elderly landlady, sat in her wicker rocker on the front porch, nursing her tea.

The screen door slipped out of his hand and thwacked against the door frame. "Sorry about that. Didn't see you sitting there."

"Got no air-conditioning in there. Cooler out here. Can't imagine how hot it's gonna be later if it's already this hot at—" She squinted up at him "—what time is it?"

"Early." Too early, considering he hadn't gotten much sleep last night. The red numbers on the digital clock by his bed read a blurry four-something by the time he left Miss Wittmer's and climbed into bed. Despite assigning another officer to check in on the Lapp farm, he felt unsettled.

What was it about the brown-eyed beauty that had gotten under his skin? And what kind of danger was she in with John Lapp still out there?

Spencer eased down, balancing his coffee and sat on the top step. Mrs. Greene spoiled him. She brewed the best coffee and left a to-go mug on the hall table inside the front door every morning. She claimed she missed having her boys around. All of them had grown and moved on with their lives, leaving her to dote over the tenants of her two upstairs apartments, only one of which was occupied.

"You finally meeting some people in this town? Doing things besides work?" Mrs. Greene had a say-whatever's-on-her-mind way of talking that didn't always allow room for him to get a word in edgewise.

Smiling, Spencer lifted his coffee and inhaled its rich scent. "Last night was work."

Mrs. Greene made a tsking noise. "How are you ever going to have a life if all you do is work?"

Spencer leaned back on the railing and shifted to look at Mrs. Greene. "I need to find you a hobby so you don't pay so much attention to me."

"Someone's got to pay attention to a handsome man like you. You can't tell me you haven't found one pretty woman in Apple Creek who you'd like to take for a nice Friday fish fry."

Spencer laughed, nearly choking on his coffee. "Is that what women like to do around here? Go to a fish fry?"

"That's what they did in my day." Mrs. Greene seemed to go somewhere for a minute before snapping out of it. "Nice crispy haddock and tartar sauce. Yum."

Spencer watched the content expression on Mrs. Greene's face. The look of a woman who had lived a good life and was now satisfied to sit back and watch the world go by—and to micromanage his.

"That girl you left behind in Buffalo hasn't come to her senses yet?"

Why had he told Mrs. Greene about Vicki? Because she had a way of prying things out of people, that's why. Spencer shook his head and rolled his eyes, feeling very much like a schoolboy under the inquisitive gaze of his grandmother, who always had an interest in everything he did. Unlike his parents, whose only interests involved all the things they required him to do.

"I've been here a year. I don't think she's suddenly going to show up at my door."

Mrs. Greene thrummed the pads of her fingers on the arm of her wicker chair. "Country's not her thing, you say?"

"Vicki was definitely a city girl." And last he heard, she was engaged to a surgeon. So very Vicki. Looked like she was going to get everything she wanted out of life.

He and Victoria had both been in law school when they started dating. She told him she had signed up for one kind of life, and Spencer had turned the tables on her by signing up for the Buffalo police exam.

"Heard she's engaged," Spencer found himself saying.

"I'm sorry."

He narrowed his gaze and stared at the long

strands of grass growing up around the railing posts where the lawn service had forgotten to trim. "I'm not. Now I don't have to feel guilty for stringing her along for so many years."

Mrs. Greene made a disagreeable sound. "That's not like you to string someone along. Don't be so hard on yourself."

It was tough not to be hard on himself when even his own father claimed disappointment. His father had been a police officer, but he had wished something more for his son. Spencer was the first college graduate in the family. A lawyer—a nice, stable, *safe* profession.

Spencer grabbed the railing and pulled himself to his feet. "Maybe it's time I got back into the game." Miss Wittmer's pretty face came to mind. He smiled wickedly at Mrs. Greene. "Maybe I should find me a nice Amish woman."

Mrs. Greene's eyes flared wide. She waved her hand in dismissal. "Don't be getting any crazy thoughts. The Amish don't take to the English. Not for datin'."

Spencer felt a smile pulling on his lips. He walked over and tapped Mrs. Greene's knee. "No, no crazy thoughts. I'll just stick to my job."

And his job was to make sure nothing happened to Miss Wittmer and her two nieces out there on the Lapp farm. Until he had John Lapp in custody, he feared he wouldn't be getting much sleep.

He couldn't screw this up. Not like he had let

down Daniel, the teenage boy in Buffalo who had ended up another grim statistic. He wouldn't let that happen again. Not on his watch.

THREE

Hannah slipped back into the house after visiting her mother in time to find Emma coming down the stairs in her sleeping gown, one hand on her doll, the other fisted and rubbing her eyes. Sarah came down only when it seemed hunger had gotten the best of her.

After feeding her nieces breakfast of, in their opinion, too-lumpy oatmeal and runny *dippy ecks*, Hannah had the girls get dressed then ushered them outside. She needed to check on the farm animals and thought perhaps the outdoors would brighten the young girls' dispositions.

Hannah reached the door of the barn as the sun was haloing the roofline of the gray, weatherworn barn. Sarah and Emma seemed content to plop down on the slight incline leading toward the barn and drag long strands of grass through their fingers. As long as the young girls stayed close to the barn, there was nothing they could get into. The freedom the Amish children had to explore was far different than the constantly monitored existence of English children.

A little voice in her head warned her that her non-motherly way of thinking was likely to get her—or her new charges—into trouble. She considered taking each by the hand and advising them to stay close, then decided it was best not to draw attention to her slipping into the barn to check on the animals.

With two hands, she peeled back the door and stepped inside. The familiar smell of manure assaulted her nose even though the barn had been swept clean yesterday for her sister's funeral. She lifted her apron to her nose, wondering how she had ever gotten used to such a foul smell. Glancing over her shoulder, she saw Emma and Sarah kicking a volleyball back and forth. Their long blond hair dangled down their backs.

The morning light filtered through the slats of the barn. The cow mooed as if happy to see her. A neighborhood boy, Samuel, had come over both in the mornings and afternoons to milk the cow and feed the horse the past few days. Samuel had told her he couldn't come this morning, but he'd be available this afternoon.

Planting her hands on her hips, she let out a heavy sigh. Even though John's move away from farming for a living had been a point of contention for her sister, Hannah was grateful. Now she only had to worry about a few animals and no crops.

Seemed a shame, though, considering all this land her family's property sat on.

Hannah grabbed a milking stool and sat. She glanced at her soft hands, now foreign to the rigors of physical labor. A shadow crossed the open door, and Hannah's hand immediately went to her head. She had taken the time to twist her hair into a messy bun, but she wasn't wearing her cap.

"*Gut* morning." The words flowed naturally from her mouth. She held up her hand to block the sun as a man strolled into the barn.

"Morning, Miss Wittmer." The casual, warm greeting brought her up short.

"Sheriff Maxwell." Hannah drew in a deep breath and found herself wishing she had on her English wardrobe complete with a little eyeliner and smoothing hair gel. She lowered her hand and forced a smile. "We have to stop meeting like this."

"Call me Spencer."

"Then you'll have to call me Hannah." She scrambled to her feet then looked past him to see her nieces hanging on to the door frame, studying the visitor.

"Go back to playing, girls. The sheriff won't be here long."

"No, I won't." Spencer shifted his stance. "Is there anyone who can take care of the animals for a while?"

"Why?"

"I think it would be safer if you and the girls left the farm for a while. Until we get this all sorted out."

"I can't pick up and leave." She lowered her voice and leaned closer to him. "This is the only home my nieces have known. They lost their mother. And my mom lives next door…and I don't know off-hand who could care for the animals full-time." Her brain swirled with all the responsibilities.

"Sounds like you have a lot of reasons to stay."

"I have a lot to figure out." Outside the barn, her nieces returned to their seats on the grassy incline and plucked long blades of grass and twisted them around their fingers.

"Maybe you can find other family to stay with the girls until we locate John and figure out what's going on here."

"My sister was all I had. As far as reaching out to other Amish families, I won't be welcomed."

"I'm sure a family would welcome your nieces."

His words felt like a knife stabbing her heart. "I'm not going to leave my nieces." She had promised her sister she'd make sure the girls were cared for. Hannah couldn't run away.

Spencer studied her with unnerving intensity. Then he snapped out of it and jerked his thumb toward the cow. "Didn't mean to interrupt your morning chores. You can milk a cow?"

She laughed, genuinely laughed, for the first time since she had received word of her sister's death. "I'm certainly capable of milking a cow or two."

She tucked a wayward strand of hair behind her ear. "This is the first morning I've had to deal with farm life since I arrived. I'm facing one thing at a time. First my nieces, then the farm animals."

"All God's creatures."

Hannah stared at him for a minute. The smile lines at the corners of his eyes softened all his features. Yet his broad chest and solid arms would intimidate any criminal. She scooped up a metal bucket, fully aware that he was watching her. "An Amish boy has been helping me. That's one thing you can say about the Amish. They always look after their own."

"They do." The two simple words held more weight than she dare explore.

She shifted the solid milking bucket from one hand to the other. She patted the backside of the cow, running her hand over its coarse fur. "How do you feel about a city slicker milking you?" The cow shuffled its back feet and let out a deep moo that vibrated through her chest. Hannah patted the animal again. "I'll take that as a yes."

Hannah pulled up a stool and straddled it. Out of the corner of her eye, she noticed Spencer standing close. Did he doubt her abilities? Inwardly she laughed. What did *he* know about farm life?

Hannah glanced at the empty bucket to make sure it was clean enough for fresh cow's milk. Three tiny holes marred the bottom of the metal bucket. The milk would leak out.

She put the bucket down and stood. She brushed past Spencer, his clean scent mixing in with fresh hay and too-fresh manure. She picked up a second pail from a nearby table. It also had several neat holes in the bottom, as if someone had taken a nail and driven it through the metal with a hammer.

"Something wrong?" Spencer's voice sounded from behind her.

Biting her lip, she turned the pail over. Bold red letters spelled out the word *English*. A red slash cut across the entire bottom of the pail, as if to say, *No English Allowed*.

Her knees grew weak. Suddenly, the heavy cotton of her Amish dress clung to her neck, strangling her. She pushed past Spencer and returned to the first pail and found the same thing. She shoved the pail into Spencer's chest.

"Look. The person who slashed my tires was busy last night."

Spencer's brow furrowed as he glanced down at the bucket in his hands.

"You have to find John. If it's John who's doing this," she quickly added. "He mustn't be in his right mind." Hannah tugged on her bun to loosen it. "To kill my sister and now try to chase me away. What does he hope to accomplish?"

"I can't speculate on his motive." Spencer inspected the pail. "We're doing everything we can to find him. To get answers."

"Maybe it's just kids. A prank..." Even as she

said it, she doubted it. But John…that didn't seem right, either. The thought of spending another long, restless night in this house made her wish she had the ability to speed up time. There were no locks on the doors, but maybe she could move furniture in front of the doors at night. She said a silent prayer in hopes of calming her frazzled nerves.

She bowed her head then lifted it and met his gaze directly. "I refuse to abandon my nieces. Because—" she swiped the bucket out of his hand "—that's exactly what he wants me to do."

When Spencer emerged from the barn a half step behind Hannah, the little girls were each holding an Amish woman's hand. The girls tugged and pulled on the woman's arm as she marched directly toward them, an expression, a combination of disgust and scolding on her plain features.

"There you are," she said, narrowing her gaze at Hannah. "These girls have been wandering around half-dressed."

"They are perfectly dressed." Hannah fingered the older girl's blond curls. "If it's their hair you're concerned with, I didn't have a chance to do their braids yet. I wasn't expecting visitors." Hannah touched her own messy bun.

The woman's gaze shot to Spencer, and her nose twitched.

"Morning. I'm Sheriff Maxwell." He held out

his hand then let it drop when it was obvious the woman wasn't going to accept it.

The woman sniffed the air. "I'm Fannie Mae Lapp." She lifted the girls' hands. The pout on the older girl's face was unmistakable. The younger of the two was on the verge of tears. "I'm the girls' *aenti*." She glared at him as if he were going to challenge her claim.

"Is there a problem, Sheriff?" He recognized Lester Lapp, John's brother, strolling across the grass. Lester had been his father's, the bishop's, guard dog, not allowing law enforcement to speak to anyone in the Lapp family since Ruth's death and John's disappearance. Lester strode down the slight incline from the house to the barn, his arms swinging confidently by his sides. "I came out as soon as we heard you were here. The bishop is also here." His tone held a warning. "If you have news regarding my brother, you can share it with me. My father is still weak from grief."

"I have no news about John." Spencer wasn't about to share news of Ruthie's murder in front of her daughters. "But I'm afraid we've had some—" he glanced down at the girls "—*events* on the property that need to be addressed." Spencer crossed his arms. "It's best if we don't talk in front of the children."

"Girls, run up to the house for me." Hannah tossed the metal bucket on the hard-packed mud.

It tumbled and landed with the graffiti facing away from the guests.

Lester gave Fannie Mae a subtle nod, giving her permission to take the children up to the house. The older niece yanked her hand from her aunt's grip and ran ahead. The little one seemed tired of being led around, reminding Spencer of a rag doll dangling by a boneless arm.

"What's going on?" Lester fingered his unkempt beard and kept his eyes trained on Hannah. "Sheriff Maxwell seems to be spending a lot of time on my brother's farm. I'd hate for the neighbors to start talking. There is much work to be done if you expect to be accepted in Apple Creek." He was speaking directly to Hannah.

Was Hannah planning on joining the Amish community permanently? Something in Spencer's heart shifted, and he wasn't proud of himself. Regardless of his initial attraction to this spunky woman, she had to make a decision that was best for her even if it meant there would be zero chance of a *them*. His disappointment seemed silly considering they had only just met. However, there was something about her simple, straightforward manner that was the complete opposite of high-maintenance Vicki.

"Lester, I'm going to forgive your bad manners on account of your tremendous loss," Hannah said, not mincing words.

"I don't need your forgiveness." A vein bulged in Lester's forehead.

"What's going on here?" Bishop Lapp navigated his way down the slope with his cane. He looked warm in his black overcoat as the sun climbed higher in the sky.

Lester's expression immediately softened. He met his father and guided him to the dirt-packed entrance of the barn.

"I have difficult news," Spencer said. The bishop had aged dramatically these past few days. Spencer cleared his throat and then told Lester and Bishop Lapp of the suspicious circumstances surrounding Ruth's death.

"Are you saying John hurt Ruth?" Lester crossed his arms over his chest, one of his fingers snagging on his suspenders. "*Neh*, impossible." He shook his head adamantly for emphasis. "It was an accident. A tragic accident."

"I'm afraid the medical examiner's findings contradict that."

"And you? How do you feel?" Lester asked.

"I have more questions than answers right now. I need to talk to John. Have you heard from him?" Spencer watched their expressions carefully, trying to detect deceit.

Lester tipped his head, hiding his eyes behind the brim of his straw hat. "*Neh*. We're worried."

"My son had nothing to do with his wife's death." The bishop narrowed his gaze. He reached out and clutched a post to steady himself. "You haven't been in town long, Sheriff. But one thing you must already know. The Amish are a peaceful people. This medical examiner...he is wrong."

"Someone slashed my tires last night." Hannah stepped forward. "Any idea who would do that?"

"It wasn't John. He hasn't been around. Don't you think if my brother was around, he'd be consoling his children? He must not be in his right mind due to grief. There's no other reason he'd stay away so long." Lester took off his straw hat and rubbed his head. "None of this makes sense. What reason would John have to hurt Ruth and then come back and destroy property?"

Spencer watched Lester. The man appeared genuinely distraught. "You're all under tremendous stress right now. I'm not accusing anyone of anything. It's my job to uncover the truth."

"We want the truth, too." The bishop's voice sounded shaky as he mopped his brow with a handkerchief.

"Do you have any idea where John might have gone? Someplace he feels comfortable. Safe."

"He felt safest here at home." A tall Amish man with broad shoulders ambled toward them. Spencer recognized him from around town. "Can't imagine what would keep my good friend away when his daughters need him." A look of disgust swept across the man's face as he took in Hannah before his features smoothed into an appropriate look of solemnity. Or had Spencer imagined it?

Spencer held out his hand. "I'm Sheriff Maxwell."

The man nodded but didn't take his hand. "I know who you are." He looped his thumbs through his suspenders. "I'm Willard Fisher. I live down the road where it meets Plum Crossing. John and I help each other out when we can. My boy Samuel has been caring for the animals while he's gone." He shook his head in disbelief. "I was away visiting family in Ohio. I wish I had been here to console him after his wife's accident."

Lester puffed out his chest, as if in competition with the new arrival. "My brother was overcome with grief. He found his wife's body. I can't imagine what I'd do under the circumstances."

"Have faith." Willard's mouth flattened into a grim line. "Have faith in *Gott* and continue on."

"Do you know if John or Ruth had issue with anyone? Someone who might have wanted to hurt her?" Spencer shifted his stance, feeling as if he had to brace himself against the men's displeasure.

The bishop shook his head. "We lead simple lives."

"Are you saying Ruth's death wasn't an accident?" Willard frowned.

"That's exactly what I'm saying."

Willard and Lester glanced at one another

while Hannah looked like she was tired of holding her tongue.

Spencer's cell phone rang. He glanced at its display. "I have to get this. Excuse me." As he stepped away, the back of his head prickled with the men's laser-like gazes.

Hannah picked up the metal bucket and hung it upside down on the post near the barn. She watched the men to see if anyone had a reaction to the graffiti written on the bottom of the bucket.

"Don't let your English ways interfere with our peaceful life here." Lester's fiery gaze slid from the sheriff to her.

Willard crossed his arms over his broad chest, but didn't say anything. He obviously agreed. No one wanted an outsider living in their midst. She could dress up in her dead sister's clothes, but no one would truly accept her until she embraced the Amish way and was baptized and found a suitable Amish husband.

Hannah's pulse whooshed in her ears. "My sister was murdered. You can't ignore that. The sheriff has to do a thorough investigation. If John was involved, you can't protect him."

Lester shook his head. "My brother had nothing to do with Ruth's tragic death. It was an accident."

Hannah lifted her trembling hands to dismiss him. "I can't listen to this."

She strode past Lester. He hollered after her,

"Will you be joining us for church service tomorrow? We are having service in our home."

Hannah turned and tugged on the collar of her dress. The thought of sitting in a sweaty barn for three hours listening to Bishop Lapp talk did not appeal to her, but she knew she had to make an effort on account of the girls. Her air-conditioned church back in Buffalo had spoiled her. It wasn't God she was opposed to, it was falling back into her old Amish lifestyle before she made a true decision. Things were happening so fast.

"I have a lot of work to do around here," she muttered, her brain racing for an excuse.

"It's Sunday," the bishop said. "A day of rest."

"John and Ruth would want the children to go to church service," Lester piled on.

Low blow.

"I'm not sure how I would get there." Her car wasn't an option even if her tires weren't slashed.

"My family can take the girls," Willard offered.

Hannah's gaze shifted to the stern man and wondered where his son Samuel had gotten his soft-spoken demeanor. "I can take the girls to the service. *Denki.*" The Pennsylvania Dutch word for *thank you* slipped out of her mouth so naturally it caught her off guard. She'd take the horse and buggy, something she hadn't done for years.

Hannah thought she detected a low chuckle from Willard, and her cheeks immediately fired hot.

"We look forward to seeing you there." The

bishop tapped the earth with his cane to empha-
size his point. "You cannot live in two worlds."

"I'm doing my best," Hannah said. "My priority
is caring for my nieces."

Willard picked up the bucket and turned it over,
studying the graffiti. "You found this in the barn?"

Hannah swallowed around a knot in her throat.
"Yes, seems someone wants me to leave."

Willard hung the bucket back on the post.
"Shame to ruin a perfectly good bucket." He turned
and looked at Hannah. "Is my son doing the chores
to your satisfaction?"

"Samuel's been a big help, thank you." Hannah
felt the need to defend Samuel, and she wasn't sure
why. "I hope his helping me here hasn't caused you
more work on your own farm."

"You need the help. John will be home soon, then
Samuel will be back on my farm." Willard said it
so matter-of-factly, she wondered if he knew something she didn't.

Unexpected emotion rolled over Hannah. She
lowered her voice. "I do hope John comes home
soon and this—whatever this is—is all cleared up."

"He will," the bishop said. "It's best if you follow the *Ordnung* while you are here. I do not want
my granddaughters to be influenced by worldly
things. I will pray that once you are settled, you
will decide to bend a knee." The bishop made a few
shuffle steps to turn around. He picked each step
deliberately as he walked toward the house. A knot

twisted her stomach. Would she ever be ready to be baptized in the Amish church?

Lester stepped forward. His features softened, yet the angle of his mouth seemed strained. "Fannie Mae and I will raise Emma and Sarah. *Gott* has not yet blessed us with children."

A mix of relief, apprehension and dread washed over Hannah. Lester had offered her a way out.

"This life isn't for you. You can return to Buffalo. We'll take care of the girls." Lester hesitated a fraction. "Until John is back and fit to care for them."

Uncomfortable, Hannah glanced behind Lester and noticed Spencer sitting on the porch steps talking animatedly to the girls. They had bright smiles on their faces, the first she had seen since returning to Apple Creek.

Hannah refocused on Lester. "If I left the girls in your care, could I visit them?"

A muscle pulsed in his jaw. "*Neh.* Your life in the outside world would only confuse them. Raising her children here was important to Ruth. Ruth is gone, but don't take her children away from everything that is important to them."

Hannah hated Lester's message, but she knew he was right. She backed away from him and made a show of swiping imaginary hay from her skirt. "I'll have to think about it."

"Fannie Mae will be a good *mem* to them."

Hannah's gaze drifted to Lester's wife, standing

apart as Spencer played with the two girls. Perhaps the woman didn't know how to interact with children because she didn't have any of her own. Indecision weighed heavily on Hannah, sucking the air out of her lungs.

"You should give this serious consideration." Lester adjusted his straw hat by its brim. "I believe *Gott* has bigger plans for me in this community. I don't want my family distracted by the outside world."

"*Gott* decides such things. Not man. Be humble," Willard scolded Lester.

Lester bristled. Perhaps Lester, like Hannah, had forgotten Willard was standing within earshot.

Hannah ran a hand across the back of her neck. "You want me to leave and to leave quietly?"

Lester's dark eyes bored into her. "I want what's best for my brother's children."

"My sister would want me to be their guardian."

"The children still have a guardian. *Their father.*" Lester's eyebrows disappeared under his hat.

"I will be their guardian until that matter is settled." Hannah bustled past Lester and strode up the hill. The ache in her brain pounded in time with her racing heart.

"Everything okay?" Spencer stood when Hannah reached the porch. The compassion in his eyes diffused a fraction of her anger. Six-year-old Emma jumped to her feet to stand next to Spencer, looking up at him with big blue eyes as trusting as her *mem*'s.

Hannah glanced at Fannie Mae quickly, then back at Spencer. "Everything is great. Girls, would you like some fresh-baked muffins?" Hannah wanted to make up for the lumpy oatmeal from earlier, but feared her baking skills were also rusty.

Emma and Sarah raced Hannah inside. The screen door slammed in its frame, shutting out the outside world, even if only temporarily.

FOUR

Hannah adjusted the buckle on the horse's harness and tugged on the end of the leather strap. Quietly, she muttered to Buttercup, reassuring her sister's beautiful horse as she hitched the animal to the buggy. This was the second time she'd done this in the past twenty-four hours, and it was beginning to feel like old hat.

Hannah had done a lot of reflecting since yesterday's church service. It had been more than a decade since she'd sat on the backless benches at an Amish service, praying and singing the hymns from the *Ausbund*. The language she had tried to put behind her when she moved to Buffalo came back with ease. She felt a certain peace she hadn't felt in a while. A peace she struggled to find as an outsider in the English word. Yet she didn't know if she'd be able to commit to the Amish way.

Would she ever be ready?

Hannah had no idea. But for now, she had to get answers. No one other than the sheriff wanted to entertain the idea that John might have played a role in her sister's death. She had decided if anyone truly knew John, it was his friend Willard. Willard was one of the men who had left Apple Creek with John and later returned. She had learned this much from her mother last night.

And something about Willard sent Hannah's nerves on edge.

Hannah adjusted the final strap on the horse's harness and stepped back to admire her work. Hitching a horse to a buggy took a lot more time and effort than hopping into her car and jamming the key into the ignition. But there was something very satisfying about it.

Hannah had left Emma and Sarah and some building blocks with her mother, promising she wouldn't be long. She patted Buttercup's mane when she was done hitching her to the buggy, satisfied that some tasks, however complicated, came naturally. She wondered if her ex-boyfriend back in Buffalo would call her inept now? No, more than likely he'd be too busy mocking her choice of clothing.

Wow. She hadn't thought about him since she got the phone call about her sister. Maybe she had moved on. Too bad it took her sister's death for her to do so.

A cool breath prickled the hair at the back of her neck despite the warm summer sun beating down on her. She glanced around the deserted farm.

Hannah hustled into the buggy. "Trot," she commanded the horse. The buggy bobbled and dipped over the ruts. She smiled to herself with satisfaction. Willard lived in walking distance—Samuel walked back and forth most days to do his chores—but Hannah hoped she'd have time after talking to Willard to run into town to pick up a few necessities.

Once on the country road, Hannah flicked the reins, and the horse picked up his gait. The country air caressed her face. The fresh smell of cut grass at a nearby home tickled her nose, and the warm sun kissed her face. She had forgotten how peaceful it was to be out on a country road all alone.

Except for the occasional car or truck whizzing by.

Beyond the curve, she saw Willard's place. She tugged on Buttercup's reins and pulled off the main road. She hopped out of the buggy and looped the reins around a post on the split rail fence lining the front of their property. As she walked toward the front door, her heart raced wildly. She didn't know what she was going to say to this man. She couldn't very well come out and ask him if he thought his friend was a murderer. Willard didn't exactly exude what she'd call the warm fuzzies.

Apprehension made her footsteps deliberate. Maybe she should let Spencer handle the investigation. But Willard was unlikely to talk to someone in law enforcement. She straightened her back and climbed the last step. Perhaps he would be more open with an Amish woman, a hesitant one at that.

Hannah lifted her hand to knock and stopped when she saw her old friend Rebecca walking toward the door. The shocked expression on her friend's face surely matched the one on her own. "I heard you were back, Hannah." Rebecca made no effort to open the screen door.

"Rebecca, what are you doing here?" Hannah took a step back, wondering if she had gotten the wrong house. "I'm looking for Willard Fisher."

"My husband is doing chores in the barn." Rebecca glanced behind her, fidgeting with the fabric of her skirt.

"You're married to Willard? But his son…" Her words drifted off. Samuel was too old to be her dear friend's child.

"I am the boy's stepmother. His mother died when he was very young. Samuel is like my own."

The word *oh* formed and died on Hannah's lips. "But you weren't with him at the church service yesterday."

"My youngest was ill. I kept both little ones home." As if on cue, two small children ran up and clung to their mother's skirt. Rebecca gently touched one head, then the other. "This is Katie and Grace."

Hannah smiled. Nostalgia edged her grief. *This* was the life she had walked away from. "Hi, girls."

She lifted her gaze to their mother. "May I speak with Willard? Perhaps I can go to the barn."

"No, he doesn't like to be disturbed." Rebecca pushed open the front door with her bare foot. Behind her, the girls peered around their mother. "I suppose he won't mind if you come in and wait a minute. He should be in for lunch soon." Rebecca spun on her heel. Hannah followed her to the kitchen where Rebecca continued to make lunch, but didn't offer Hannah a seat or anything to drink.

Hannah decided this must be what it felt like to be shunned.

"Go wash your hands," Rebecca said to the little ones.

The two children, Hannah guessed, were around five or six. Close to Emma's age. She wondered if they were friendly with her nieces. She was about to ask them when they spun around and ran away, presumably to wash their hands.

"I'm sorry about Ruthie."

"Thank you." Hannah cleared her throat, eager to change subjects. "Samuel has been a big help to me on the farm."

Rebecca nodded. "I suppose there's not much to do on the farm nowadays with John working down the way." Her friend was too polite to make mention of the fact that currently John wasn't working anywhere.

Hannah touched her cap, suddenly self-conscious. "I suppose it's true. There are no crops to worry about, but the animals still need care. I appreciate Samuel's help."

Rebecca nodded again. She put aside the knife she had been using to spread the apple butter on bread and said, "Ruthie was like a sister to me."

"Ruthie felt the same way about you." Guilt snuck up and twisted Hannah's insides. "I'm sorry I left Apple Creek without saying goodbye to you. You had always been a dear friend."

Her friend shrugged and turned back around and continued to prepare her family's lunch.

Hannah leaned her shoulder on the door frame. "I couldn't tell you I was leaving. I couldn't tell anyone."

Rebecca turned around with a spoon in her hand. Something red from the spoon plopped onto the floor. The hurt expression on her friend's face wounded her. "I thought we were *gut* friends. It wonders me why you snuck away from Apple Creek in the middle of the night. I never imagined you a fence jumper. The bishop, your parents, everyone came to me with questions." Rebecca drew in a shuddering breath on the verge of tears. "I didn't have any answers."

"That's why I couldn't tell you. I didn't want to put you in that position." Hannah tugged on the collar of her Amish dress. Right now she longed for cooler English clothes and air-conditioning.

Rebecca turned around and resumed preparing the lunches. "*Yah* well, I thought you were happy here."

"I wasn't." Hannah didn't tell her friend about her father's verbal abuse. And how could she explain her discontent with a life her friend embraced?

"I wish you had told me." Rebecca's words were so soft Hannah had to strain to hear them.

The back door slammed, and Willard stomped into the kitchen. He came up short when he saw Hannah. He spun around and told Samuel to grab his sisters and go back outside. Something flickered across his face and then disappeared. A bead of sweat rolled down Hannah's back.

Willard glared accusingly at his wife. "You have a visitor?"

"I'm here to see you." Hannah quickly spoke up, not wanting her friend to get into trouble.

"Do you have news regarding John?" Willard asked, his voice gruff.

"No, I was hoping to ask you about John. I know you were good friends. How was he? I mean, before Ruthie died?"

Willard washed his hands in the sink, dried them on a towel and then hung the towel on a wood peg. "*Gut.*"

Hannah smoothed a hand across her bib. "My sister was worried about him."

"You spoke with Ruth?" Willard's tone was strangely flat.

Hannah nodded, feeling like a fifteen-year-old who had been caught kissing a boy behind the barn, not a grown woman who had every right to spend time with her sister. "We met a few times and chatted. We're family. We missed each other."

Willard pulled out a chair and slammed the legs down on the floor. Rebecca flinched. "You made your choice when you left Apple Creek."

"Hannah just lost her sister. Don't be…" Rebecca deflated under her husband's withering stare. Rebecca had swiftly come to her defense often when they were kids. It had been Rebecca, Ruthie and Hannah. The three musketeers. The only consolation Hannah had when she left was that Ruthie still had Rebecca. But it seemed now Willard had Rebecca and kept a tight rein on her.

"Don't be…what?" Willard repeated.

Rebecca seemed to swallow hard to gather her nerve. "Hannah made a bad decision when she left Apple Creek, but we can have compassion now as she deals with her sister's death. Perhaps this is *Gott*'s way of bringing her back home."

Hannah stifled a grimace at the notion God had used her sister's murder to bring her back into the fold.

"We need to find forgiveness," Rebecca added.

"Are you looking for forgiveness?" Willard picked up his spoon and scooped up a mouthful of soup, never taking his eyes off Hannah.

"I am here to find out about John." She struggled to keep her jaw from trembling.

Willard dabbed his mouth with a napkin. "John seemed fine. He was a hardworking Amish man dedicated to his family. We both had lost our way, much like you—" she knew he had to get a dig in there "—but we had both come to realize living apart from the temptations of the outside world was the way our parents and their parents before them wanted things."

"I can't believe Ruthie's gone." Rebecca turned and filled four more bowls and set them on the table across from her husband.

Willard flattened his palms on the table on either side of his soup bowl. "Rebecca can mind Emma and Sarah Lapp until their father returns. I understand you have a job in Buffalo you have to get back to."

Hannah did a double take. The Amish grapevine was amazing.

"I am capable of caring for my nieces." Hannah hiked her chin.

Rebecca watched her husband carefully. She stood behind her chair, waiting for something, and then Hannah realized she was preventing her friend from eating.

"I better go."

Rebecca led her to the door and whispered, "I'm sorry I couldn't invite you to stay for lunch. Willard is quite strict and believes we should stay separate from the English. No exceptions." Her voice wavered. "I'm sorry."

Hannah brushed the back of her friend's hand. "But it's me, Rebecca." Her friend seemed unmoved, so Hannah nodded. "It's okay."

Rebecca retreated into the house, and Hannah could hear her calling the children in to eat. Loneliness weighed heavily on her, and she swallowed down a lump of grief in her throat.

Forever the outsider.

Each day was running into the next, and Hannah struggled to remember what day it was. She rolled out of bed and pulled on jeans and a sweatshirt, figuring no one would see her at this hour. 5:00 a.m. was horribly early to have responsibilities like farm animals. Samuel had told her yesterday he had to help his father on the farm this morning, but he'd do his best to stop by and help in the afternoon. Part of her wondered if Willard just wanted to make it more difficult for her so she'd be forced to concede.

However, to be fair, the Fishers had a farm of their own to run.

Hannah gave herself a pep talk and splashed cold water on her face. She better get used to getting up this early if she planned on staying. *If.* She slipped her cell phone into her back pocket. It gave her a sense of security. She was grateful she had thought to bring the car charger for her phone. She still hadn't gotten used to being out in the country in the middle of nowhere, and she hadn't installed the locks on the house, a small part of her fearing she'd be breaking the rules and giving the elders another reason to ask her to leave. In the darkness of early morning, her reasoning sounded silly. She had to keep her nieces safe.

She stalked quietly through the darkened house. She grabbed the flashlight from the kitchen counter and stepped outside, pulling the door closed behind her. A warm summer breeze carried the farm scents of her childhood and with it not nostalgia but a longing for something more. A longing that had grown from her preteen years into her teen years, into something she couldn't dismiss. Something bigger that could only be found beyond the fences of the Amish community.

But *had* she found more in her boring job in Buffalo? A feeling of acceptance, of belonging, eluded her. Her condescending former boyfriend and her roommates didn't understand or want to understand her conservative ways. Hannah had found cheap rent near the university, but not like minds.

Hannah glanced toward her mother's residence. Dark, just as she expected it to be. She wondered, not for the first time, if the Lapp family would care for her mother if Hannah returned to Buffalo. The Amish rallied around one another, right?

Her mind drifted a lot in the early-morning quiet hours. She remembered Ruthie—during their

secretive meetings over French fries and shakes—
telling her how wonderful it would be for the girls
to know their aunt. For Hannah to one day get married and raise her family nearby. If only Hannah
would come back to Apple Creek and be baptized.

A wave of guilt slammed into Hannah. Why had
she been so quick to brush off her sister's request?
What if Hannah had returned? Would she have
seen the deteriorating relationship between Ruthie
and John and been able to intervene? If that had
indeed been the case.

Hannah grimaced when her sneaker hit something smooshie as she entered the barn. She lifted
up her foot and noticed a dark shadow of who-
knows-what. She groaned. She *so* wasn't cut out for
this. The bishop's words scraped across her brain.
All she had to do was turn her nieces over to their
aunt and uncle, and she could return to her regular life.

Her regular life.

No cow dung. No horses. No predawn chores.

Her boring, unfulfilled, regular life.

She had escaped the Amish life only to find her
life still unfulfilled.

She shook her head and kept moving forward.
The cow mooed halfheartedly, and she patted his
backside. "That's how I feel, too, buddy."

Hannah turned on a kerosene lamp, spreading a
warm, yellow glow across the barn.

She knew how to milk a cow by hand—one of

the perks of growing up on a farm—but she had gotten accustomed to running to the grocery store for a gallon of milk. For the past decade, her biggest concern with milk had been making sure she consumed it before the expiration date. Which wasn't always an easy task when she was the only one drinking it.

Hannah pulled up a stool and talked to the cow reassuringly. She had found a usable pail in the far corner of the barn.

A crash—the tinkling of breaking glass— sounded behind her. The barn was immediately cast into darkness. She froze and swallowed her growing panic. Her thumping heart drowned out the silence.

"Is someone there?" she croaked out.

A crackle. Then another.

Fear swept across her arms, and sweat pooled down her back. She grabbed the flashlight next to her stool and directed it toward where she had placed the lamp. The kerosene lamp had crashed onto the barn floor. The flammable liquid spread across the loose hay scattered on the floor.

Panic edged out all rational thought.

Fire! The animals!

Hannah bolted past the flames. She had to do something. Then as if by divine intervention, she remembered the blanket in the barn near Buttercup's stall.

She grabbed the blanket, the heavy, scruffy burlap, her only hope. Buttercup neighed in protest, as if sensing Hannah's panic. She tossed the blanket onto the flames licking across the loose hay, eager to sweep across the barn floor. She stomped on the blanket a few more times to make sure the flames were extinguished.

Shaking and unsure of herself, afraid to leave the barn in case a hot spot flared up, she reached into her back pocket and pulled out her cell phone.

If Bishop Lapp and his eldest son hadn't convinced her she had no business working this farm and caring for her nieces, this fire had.

Spencer's cell phone interrupted his dream. He couldn't recall the specifics, but he was pretty sure a real-life nightmare was haunting his dreams. He wondered if he'd ever get past that night in Buffalo.

He shook off the guilt and sleep and answered the phone with a curt, "Maxwell."

Hannah sounded equal parts frightened and embarrassed when she explained the accident that had led to a small fire. She had convinced herself, but not him, that she had extinguished it. He dressed quickly and drove out to the Lapp's farm in a record eleven minutes. After recent events, he wasn't assuming anything was an accident.

When he arrived, he found Hannah right where she said she'd be, at the door of the barn where she could keep an eye on the animals and the house where her nieces slept.

He pulled his truck onto the grass and climbed out. The sky was pink and purple with fingers of white clouds. Funny how he noticed things out here. In the city, he had forgotten to look up at the sky.

Hannah leaned against the barn door dressed in jeans and a sweatshirt, her long brown hair flowing over her shoulders. *This* was the woman he found himself drawn to, but he had to push that thought from his head. If she was going to return to her Amish roots, he didn't want to be standing there with a broken heart.

And his job was to protect her. Period.

Hannah levered off the edge of the barn door and pointed at the charred blanket on the ground. "I must have put the lamp too close to the edge. It fell over… I could have burned the entire barn down." She glanced nervously toward the house. "The wind could have carried the flames to the house. My nieces…" Anger creased her forehead. "Maybe I'm not cut out for life on a farm raising my sister's daughters. Maybe everyone is right."

Spencer inspected the charred blanket. "You were smart. You contained the fire. It's okay." He tossed the blanket outside and touched her upper arms lightly. "Look at me."

She bowed her head and sobbed quietly. Her legs seemed to go out from under her, and he wrapped his arms around her. She rested her head on his shoulder and stilled for a moment. The floral scent of her shampoo tickled his nose. He refused to let down his guard. This was strictly a professional relationship. Suddenly, as if reading his mind, she stiffened and stepped away from him, batting away at the tears that glistened on her cheeks in the morning sun.

Sirens sounded in the distance. A horrified look flashed in her eyes. "Did you alert the fire department?"

"Yes, I couldn't risk wasting precious time if the fire had gotten out of control."

"Oh, no. Now the neighbors will really be talking."

"Stop worrying about them."

"My mother!" Hannah's eyes grew wide. "I better go tell her everything's okay."

Spencer nodded then strode across the driveway to meet the fire engine. A firefighter jumped out of the truck and followed Spencer into the barn.

A few minutes later, Hannah joined him in the yard. "My mother's had to deal with a lot lately."

"Is she okay?"

Hannah nodded. "And believe it or not, Emma and Sarah are still sleeping."

"The firemen are going to saturate the area around the charred hay to make sure there're no hot spots."

"Okay."

"You've been through a lot, too. Sit down." Spencer guided her to the grassy incline.

Hannah let out a sigh. She held a fisted hand to her mouth. "I don't belong here."

"You're fine, everything's fine." Spencer rubbed her back in small circles, trying to reassure her.

"I wanted to do right by my sister. By my sister's children. But I'm not meant to run a farm." She swept her hand in the air in front of her. "I can't even commit to the wardrobe, never mind their ways." She shook her head. "I had hoped to take it day by day, but…" She threaded her fingers through her hair. "I almost burned down the barn."

Spencer tilted his head in an attempt to get her to shift her gaze from the barn to him. He was rewarded with a sad smile.

"For a city girl, you really thought fast." He stood and picked up the discarded blanket. The fire had burned two large holes into the fabric with a smattering of tiny dots. He folded it and tossed it down again.

She shrugged and hugged her knees to her chest.

Spencer scanned the barn. Something about this rubbed him the wrong way. "Did you see anyone out here this morning?"

Hannah's eyes flashed wide. "No. You think someone knocked over the lantern? Tried to burn down the barn?" She flattened her hand on her midsection and looked like she was going to be sick.

"Just the other night someone slashed your tires." He scrubbed a hand over his whiskered jaw. "Too many things to be considered a coincidence.

Listen…" She accepted his outstretched hand, and he pulled her to her feet. She swiped at the back of her jeans.

"I fear the next time someone goes after you, they aren't going to slash your tires or knock over a lantern."

"What?" The word came out as barely a whisper.

"I've seen these things escalate." First the child gets in trouble in school, then he starts hanging out with the wrong crowd, he's arrested for shoplifting, then shot in the head during a gang initiation gone bad. But that was his dark secret. His personal failure.

Not hers.

Hannah blinked at him in shock. A knot formed between his shoulder blades. Regrets haunted him. He had tried to save a young city kid, but drugs and gangs were too prevalent to spare a boy living in poverty. "I won't let anything happen to you." He had failed to keep that promise before.

Never again.

Hannah ran a hand across the back of her neck. "I'm not in any real danger, am I? The tire slashing was a prank, right?" She looked up at him, trust in her bright brown eyes.

"I'm not a fan of coincidences, remember?"

She sighed heavily. "Why would someone do this to me? If John wants me to leave, then he needs to come home, prove his innocence and raise his children." Her soft voice hardened with anger. "Besides John, I don't have enemies." She locked gazes with him. "The Amish don't believe in violence. No one from this community would try to hurt me regardless of how they feel about me personally." The hesitancy in her voice told him she wasn't buying it, either.

"John Lapp is our primary focus."

"Then he needs to show his face. Be a man." Her lower lip shook with rage.

"These are not the actions of a rational person." It was speculation, but the best idea he had right now.

Hannah threaded her fingers through her hair and closed her eyes briefly. "Maybe this fire was caused by my own carelessness." Her shoulders dropped. "I'm sorry I woke you up early. The fire had me freaked out. I was worried it would flare up again." Hannah brushed the palms of her hands together as if she had put this entire situation behind her. "It appears the fire department has taken care of that." The firefighters wrapped up their hose and tucked it away.

One of the men wandered their way. "You're good, ma'am. Just be careful with the kerosene lamps."

"I will. Thank you."

The firefighter waved to Spencer. "Take it easy, Sheriff." The firefighter climbed onto the truck. The fire engine eased out of the driveway and onto the main road.

When the fire engine was out of sight, Spencer

turned to Hannah. "We don't know the fire was an accident." They locked gazes for a long moment. "You need to be careful."

"I'm out here alone with the girls. My mother lives on the property, but her health keeps her inside most of the time. What am I supposed to do?"

"I'll make sure you're protected."

She dragged the heel of her hand across her forehead. "You can't guard me out here. You have a job."

"I'll have extra patrols come by. I won't let anything happen to you." But he had been having extra patrols and still this happened.

"Maybe it is time for me to leave."

Spencer brushed his knuckles down the sleeve of her sweatshirt. "You've had a stressful week, and I know you think you're in over your head. Don't make any rash decisions until you have a chance to consider all your options." He wanted her to be safe, but for selfish reasons he didn't want her to leave Apple Creek. A twinge of guilt pinged him.

"I better check on the girls." Hannah pulled the sleeves of her sweatshirt down around her hands. "Can I make you breakfast?"

He held up his hand, intending to refuse when Hannah added a little too breezily, "It's the least I can do for dragging you all the way out here before sunrise."

Spencer followed her to the house. When she

opened the door, they found Emma sitting in a chair hugging her plain, faceless fabric doll.

Hannah glanced at him over her shoulder. The smile slipped from her face. "Have you been up long, sweetie?"

Emma bowed her head and buried her face into the doll and squeezed its middle tight.

"The fire truck must have been scary. I promise everything is okay now." Hannah crouched in front of the little girl and smiled. "Where's your sister?"

"In bed." Emma sniffled. "I thought you were gone. Like *Mem*." Emma hid her feet under her nightgown and pulled her knees to her chest. "And I saw that big truck like when *Mem*…"

Pink blossomed on Hannah's face, and she looked as if she was fighting back tears. "Oh, no, sweetie. I went outside to do chores. Careless Aunt Hannah knocked over a lamp. That's why the firemen were here. I wouldn't leave you. Ever."

Emma looked up, hesitantly at first, then a shy smile crossed her face. She scooted to the edge of the chair and slipped her hand into Hannah's.

Spencer cleared his throat, feeling like a true outsider. "I should head out."

Hannah kissed Emma on the cheek and turned to Spencer. "I believe I owe you breakfast."

FIVE

After breakfast, Hannah and Spencer lingered over coffee while the girls returned to their dolls. Hannah wondered if her sister would have minded if she purchased the girls real dolls with blinking eyes and fancy clothes, then decided the faceless, plain ones were more suitable. For now.

Hannah set her mug down. "So, Sheriff, you know all about me, and I know nothing about you. What brings you to the sleepy town of Apple Creek?"

"The job. I got tired of being a police officer in the city. Apple Creek had an opening when the last sheriff resigned after his son was indirectly tied to the disappearance of a five-year-old Amish girl."

Hannah shuddered. "Poor sweet Mary Miller. I remember when she went missing. What a tragedy." Amish parents kept a closer eye on their children for a long time after Mary went missing while shopping at the general store with her older brother.

She lowered her gaze and said a quiet prayer for the girl's soul.

"Anytime a child is hurt or…" A faraway look flitted across his eyes. "It's the hardest part of this job."

"I can't imagine."

"Anyway…" Spencer took a deep breath, snapping out of it. "I thought a job change would be good."

Hannah narrowed her gaze. "Seems like it would be a lot more exciting to work in the city rather than coming to the aid of an Amish woman in the middle of farm country."

"Can't say I've ever helped an Amish woman in Buffalo."

"Probably not." She laughed. Something about this man lightened her heart.

"Where in Buffalo did you live?" He rarely broke eye contact when he spoke, making her self-conscious.

"I have a small apartment in the university district. I'm living there month-to-month with two roommates, both college students."

Spencer seemed to consider this a moment. A smile pulled on the corners of his lips. "I can't see you hanging out at college parties."

Hannah waved her hand. "I'm a little too old to be hanging out with the college crowd. My roommates are grad students. Not the partying type. But if you listen to them, you'd think I was the most boring person in the world."

The creases around his eyes deepened when he laughed. "I'm sure you're not *that* boring."

Hannah averted her gaze, and her cheeks grew warm. "I grew up in a very conservative lifestyle. I wasn't prepared for the things that go on in the English world." She lifted her gaze and met his.

"You just haven't met the right people yet." His smooth voice rolled over her, and she couldn't help wonder what he meant.

His intense regard unnerved her, so she reached across the table and nudged his arm in hopes of lightening the mood. "Okay, funny man. I wasn't going to pry, but tell me why you'd leave Buffalo for a town whose nearest Wegman's grocery store is a forty-five-minute drive."

Spencer leaned toward her, resting his elbows on the table. "There's more to life than the Cadillac of all grocery stores."

Hannah narrowed her eyes. "Oh, I don't know." She laughed, then grew sober. "I'm really curious about you. Why did you leave Buffalo?"

Spencer's chest rose and fell on a heavy sigh. "A police officer sees a lot working in the city." The raw honesty on his face exposed a chink in his armor. Their brief connection made her feel equally exposed.

She pushed back the chair and stood, giving him her best I'll-let-you-off-the-hook-for-now expression. "I better red up the room, as my kinfolk would say, and turn back into Amish aunt." She plucked at her sweatshirt. "Sometimes I feel like spinning around like Wonder Woman to change back and forth." She giggled. "Oh man, I'm getting punchy."

Spencer lightly touched her wrist as she passed. She paused and glanced at his tan hand against her pale skin. A feeling of being protected, safe, coiled around her heart.

"Don't let anyone pressure you into doing or being something you're not."

Hannah stared at him for a long moment. "I won't." The words sounded unconvincing even in her own ears.

Hannah cleared away the dishes and moved to the sink. She enjoyed the companionable silence as she washed, and Spencer dried. Never in a million years would her father have done what he called *women's work*. Almost done, Hannah put the frying pan under the faucet and a powerful gush sent water bouncing off the pan and into their faces.

Scrunching up her nose, Hannah turned to Spencer. The front of his brown hair was soaked, and big drips ran down his face. She grabbed the dish towel from him and dabbed at his cheeks. Laughing until her vision blurred, she apologized profusely.

After a moment, he pulled her hand away from his face. Their eyes locked, and tension stretched between them.

Spencer was the first to break the silence. "I'm fine. Really. It's just a little water."

The sound of someone clearing his throat made Hannah jump. Pinpricks of unease swept across her skin. She dropped her hands to her sides and pivoted. Lester Lapp stood in the doorway, disapproval etched on his features. His dark eyes shadowed by the brim of his straw hat.

Hannah quickly stepped away from Spencer as if she had been doing something wrong. Then she glanced down at her jeans and sweatshirt. She crossed her arms over her middle, as if she could hide her wardrobe. She felt equal parts defiant and embarrassed.

"I was out in the barn this morning. I thought it was more practical to wear these clothes than a dress." The words poured from her mouth. She felt like she was thirteen again, defending herself to her father.

"It wonders me if it would have been simpler to go out in your undergarments to avoid soiling your English clothes."

Hannah gritted her teeth. Spencer moved next to her, his shoulders squared as if to defend her. She discreetly let the back of her hand brush his thigh, a silent caution.

Lester's eyes went to her hand and an emotion—disgust, maybe?—registered on his face. The gooey-sweet voice of a woman unaccustomed to talking to children reached Hannah's ears. *Fannie Mae*.

Lester gave her a smarmy smile. "It's time Fannie Mae spent more time with the children. *Gut, yah*."

"You haven't given me a chance to make a decision." Hannah stepped forward. "I am here for the girls."

Spencer rested his hand on the small of her back, a reassuring gesture.

Lester's brow creased. "*Yah*, well, you can't even wear appropriate clothing. Fannie Mae will raise the girls as Ruth and John would have done until my brother comes home."

The simple statement sent sharp pains jabbing into Hannah's heart. She cut a sideways glance to Spencer, whose expression was hard to read.

The strong-willed part of her wanted to tell Lester to take a flying leap. To tell him in no uncertain terms that *she* was going to care for her sister's children. The practical side of her—the wounded, grieving side of her—feared he was right. She had no business raising her sister's children. She knew nothing about being a mother. Nothing about managing a farm on her own.

And worst of all, she questioned the Amish way.

Ruthie had reached out to Hannah in the final months of her life. Yet Hannah had failed to realize the seriousness of her sister's concerns. *Had Ruthie feared for her life and Hannah hadn't been able to read between the lines?* A throbbing started behind her eyes. She had let her sister down.

Hannah couldn't fail her nieces.

"The *hurrieder* we take Sarah and Emma into our home, the hurrieder they'll adjust. A delay is only making it more difficult. More confusing."

Hannah fisted her hands by her sides. She felt Spencer's gentle fingers brush against the back of her hand. "Can we talk?" he asked.

She nodded.

Spencer led her outside, down the steps and across the front lawn. "You don't have to decide right this minute."

"Maybe Lester's right. Maybe the sooner I leave, the less painful it will be for the girls." This had been the back-and-forth argument weighing in her mind for days.

Stay. Go. Stay. Go. Go. Go.

She rubbed her throbbing temple.

Spencer squared off with Hannah and angled his head to study her eyes. "Those girls love you. It doesn't have to be an all-or-nothing proposition. Considering everything that's been going on, maybe you and the girls should get away from here for a little while. Don't feel you have to hand your nieces over to Lester and Fannie Mae."

Hannah stared at him, disbelief making her breakfast roil in her stomach. "I can't leave with the girls. My sister wouldn't want that. And if I move back to Buffalo alone, Lester won't allow me to visit my nieces. They're afraid I'll be a bad influence." She shook her head. "If I decide to allow Lester and Fannie Mae to raise Sarah and Emma, I'm as good as saying goodbye. Forever."

She turned to face the road as a pickup truck zoomed by. "I'll never see them again."

"Would they really be that cruel?"

"They don't think of it as cruel. They're trying to preserve the Amish way. They interact with the outside world when necessary, but weekend visits with the black-sheep aun t would not be deemed necessary." She drew in a deep breath and let it go. Indecision crowded in on her. "Maybe life with Lester and Fannie Mae would be for the best."

"You don't have to give Lester an answer now. Think about it." Something in Spencer's tone gave her pause. Her heart kicked up a notch. Would Spencer be disappointed if she left?

Hannah strolled toward the house.

"Wait," Spencer called.

Hannah turned back slowly.

"Mrs. Greene, my landlady, has an empty apartment in the building where I live. You could take the girls there. You'd be safer."

She narrowed her gaze at him, letting his words sink in. Her lips moved, but no words formed. Could she rip the girls away from everything they've ever known? She shook her head and continued toward the house. She reached the top step of the porch and heard Fannie Mae's stern voice pierce the county quiet. "When you come to my house, we'll get rid of these scruffy dolls, now once. You don't need silly toys."

Hannah heard a smacking sound. "Stop fussing with your dress," Fannie Mae scolded.

Hannah stormed into the house, dizzy with adrenaline. She was ready to let Fannie Mae have it when the sight of the two girls clutching hands, standing in the center of the room, destroyed her. The sadness and fear on their faces spoke volumes.

Hannah had felt that fear while on the receiving end of one of her father's tirades. No one had come to her rescue.

Her heartbeat pulsing in her temples, Hannah glared at Fannie Mae then Lester. Lester stepped toward the girls and clutched Sarah's shoulder. "Stop this nonsense. It was just a small tap on your wrist. It couldn't have hurt that much. We're going to take you to your new home, now once."

Sarah pulled away from him and clutched her little sister's hand. "*Aenti* Hannah, don't leave."

The last shred of resistance around Hannah's heart shattered. She knelt in front of the girls and drew them into a hug. Not accustomed to physical displays of affection, they stiffened before melting into her embrace.

Hannah lifted her head. Lester and Fannie Mae seemed shell-shocked. "The girls *are* home."

"*Neh*, you cannot stay and live like you are."

Lester's nostrils flared as he gave her jeans and sweatshirt a once-over.

"You have no authority over me. I plan to stay here to raise the girls."

"Don't you mean until their *dat* comes home?" Lester tipped his hat, more out of habit, than a genuine goodbye. He stormed out of the house, his wife, her gown licking at her legs, followed behind in a tizzy.

Hannah's entire body trembled. She sat in the sitting room rocker. She gestured to Emma and the doll in her hand. When Emma realized what her aunt wanted, she handed the doll over with a pinched expression on her face. "I'll give it right back, sweetie." Hannah traced the stitching on the plain dress. "Your *mem* made this doll."

Emma looked down at her doll, a small smile tugging on her pink lips.

Hannah lifted her gaze to Spencer, who had come back into the house. A shudder worked its way down her spine. Was Spencer right? Was she not safe here with the girls?

The thick vein pulsing in Lester's temple came to mind.

Her sister's murder.

Her missing brother-in-law.

Would Lester have left so easily if Spencer hadn't been here? If she and the girls had been alone?

Across the room, Hannah locked gazes with Spencer. She couldn't put a single name to the emotions rolling off him. Uncertainty? Fear? Doubt? Or was she transferring to him all the emotions tangling her insides into a painful knot?

Later that day, Spencer looked across the cab of his truck at Hannah on their way into town to pick up locks for her front and back doors, and for her mother's house. She wore her sister's plain black dress and had her hair neatly pulled up and tucked under a bonnet. From regular clothes this morning to Amish clothes by lunch was quite the transformation. A part of him felt like he was dealing with a different person.

Hannah's two nieces were fastened in with seat belts in the backseat of his truck. Nine-year-old Sarah put up a surprisingly adamant fuss about getting into Spencer's truck. Her father, she claimed, would be very mad if they rode in an English car. It took some persuasion on Hannah's part, but Sarah wasn't fully buying the theory that it was okay for the Amish to ride in a vehicle, they just couldn't own or drive one. Thankfully, Emma was eager for a new adventure.

Spencer turned onto the main road, and Hannah spoke for the first time. "I appreciate your driving me into town." Hannah glanced over her shoulder and gave her nieces a quick look. "I need to be careful how I act because Lester's going to be looking for any reason to force me out." She neglected to add, "And take the girls." But Spencer knew that was her first concern.

"Your mind is made up?" Spencer cut her a sideways glance. He shouldn't care so much about the answer. But he did. She had sounded very convincing when she lashed out at Lester and told him *she* was going to raise the girls. He assumed that meant as part of the Amish community.

Hannah tugged on her seat belt and shifted to look out the window. It wasn't a fair question to ask while her nieces were listening from the backseat. He thrummed his fingers on the steering wheel. "What do we need to pick up?" His cheery tone sounded a little forced.

"Locks and a few basic necessities." Out of the corner of his eye he could see she was facing him now. "I do appreciate your help, especially with the locks, but if I'm going to do this, I have to figure out a way to do it on my own." Hannah fidgeted with the strings of her bonnet. "I can't call you every time I need a loaf of bread."

"*Mem* made our bread. We never needed to go to the store for that," Sarah whined from the backseat.

Hannah twisted to face her niece. "Maybe we can make bread together. You can show me how you and your *mem* made bread."

Tense silence expanded and filled the cab of his truck.

If Hannah was frustrated, she didn't let on. "What

do you have there?" She stretched her arm over the seat and retrieved her cell phone from Emma.

"I found it on the table in your room," Emma said with a hint of apology.

"That's okay. Do you want to see how it works?" Spencer imagined Emma nodded because Hannah stretched into the backseat to show her niece how to dial the phone. "Pretty cool, huh?"

"Can I play with it?" Emma asked with all the enthusiasm of a six-year-old.

"Sure."

"She shouldn't play with that," Sarah said, her tone filled with disgust. "You're bringing too many worldly things here."

"It's okay, your sister's curious."

"And you really need to stop wearing English clothes," Sarah added, heaping on her annoyance with her aunt.

Hannah plucked the fabric gathered around her thighs. "I suppose you're right. I can't slip into my jeans and sneakers anymore because I think they're more practical."

Spencer pulled his truck alongside the curb in front of the General Store in the center of Apple Creek. She had a look of expectation on her face. "What is it?" he asked.

"I hate to impose, but I was thinking we could drive to the next town to the superstore. I need so many things, and I'm on a tight budget."

"I'd be happy to…but—" he gestured with his

chin toward the row of shops "—I was thinking you and the girls might like some ice cream."

A click and a whoosh of fabric sounded from the backseat. Little Emma placed her chubby hands on the back of the seat and poked her face over the leather. "Can we have ice cream?"

A smile tilted Hannah's lips.

"My treat." Spencer climbed out of the vehicle before Hannah had a chance to protest. He walked around and opened her door. Hannah climbed out, looking around as if she were a fugitive. He leaned in close. "A quick ice cream cone, and I'll take you shopping in the next town."

Spencer opened the back door, and Emma scampered out, and a reluctant Sarah followed. Hannah nudged the older girl's shoulder. "What kind of ice cream do you like?"

"*Dat* says ice cream is only for special occasions."

Hannah sucked in a breath. "Well, this is a special occasion. Sheriff Maxwell is going to treat us. That's special, right?"

Sarah's expression grew pinched. For the briefest of moments, Hannah saw Ruthie in her daughter's face. Serious little Ruthie. Nostalgia formed a thick knot in her throat.

Spencer pointed to the clapboard sign mounted on the side of the ice cream shop. "Go pick your favorite flavor."

Emma bolted ahead, her little legs pumping

under her long dress. Hannah whispered to Sarah. "Go help your sister read the board."

Sarah turned up her nose. "She can read."

"Not as well as you, I imagine." Hannah's tone was calm and encouraging. Spencer figured she didn't give herself enough credit when it came to the girls.

Sarah squared her shoulders and marched after her sister as if selecting ice cream flavors was a royal hardship. The two little bonnets moved together as they studied the board.

An Amish woman walked toward them. She lifted her head and seemed to snort her disdain. After she passed, Hannah said, "See what I'm up against? How can I raise the grandchildren of the bishop without everyone thinking I'm not good enough? They'll be pressuring me to turn the girls over to Lester and Fannie Mae." Hannah sat at a nearby picnic table, a faraway expression in her eyes. "Maybe I'm doing what I'm accusing others of doing."

Spencer lowered his chin.

"Maybe I'm too judgmental. Lester's sternness and Fannie Mae's strictness are not unheard of in the Amish community. My own father was very strict, yet I want to believe deep down that he was a good man. I saw how good he could be to Ruthie. Maybe…" She traced a groove in the picnic table.

Spencer touched Hannah's hand and she froze. Looked up at him. "Lester might not be the best choice. I've heard stories about the Lapp family even before..." He was going to say your sister's murder, but he stopped himself.

Hannah's brows furrowed.

"John and Lester Lapp didn't get along." Spencer shot his gaze over to the ice cream stand. Emma and Sarah were still selecting flavors. "I was called to break up a fight between the brothers."

"A physical fight?"

Nodding, Spencer lifted a hold-on-a-minute finger.

Emma ran over to them. "May I please have a bubble gum ice cream cone with sprinkles?"

"Of course you can." Spencer dug out a twenty and handed it to Emma. "Would you like anything, Hannah?"

She shook her head. Spencer patted his belly. "I better not, either."

Emma ran back to her sister. Hannah and Spencer continued their conversation out of earshot, but close enough to keep an eye on the young girls.

"What were John and Lester fighting about?" Hannah asked, her tone chilly on the hot summer afternoon.

"They wouldn't tell me." Spencer sat across from Hannah at the picnic table, stuffing his legs under the table. "But I did some asking around. Isaac, an Amish man who works at the General Store, seems to think there was some discord between the men because the bishop was pressuring John to sell land to his brother."

"That land has been in my family..." Her words trailed off, as if realizing how much had changed since her family farmed the land.

"John had gotten away from farming, and the land was sitting idle. Lester wanted a sizable chunk to build a home and farm." Spencer leaned forward, resting his elbows on the table. "Good land. Cheap price."

Hannah's eyebrow twitched. "Perhaps that was the change Ruth feared. She never came out and said. Maybe she was afraid of losing our family's farm."

About ten feet away, Emma sat at a child's picnic bench, and her sister joined her.

"How was John in his faith?" Spencer asked, sliding over a fraction to get under the shade of the umbrella.

"Ruth had been convinced her husband was more committed than ever to the Amish faith, perhaps because of his experience in the outside world. She said he claimed he knew how bad things could be." She played with the string of her cap. "I told her things weren't all that bad in the outside world. I guess I felt a little defensive. But I didn't paint an overly glowing picture, either. I didn't want to be responsible for any unrest on her part."

"Would you say his commitment was fanatical?"

Spencer studied her face, and something flashed across her eyes. Fear? Annoyance? Confusion?

"Fanatical." Hannah seemed to be trying the word on for size. "My sister and her husband were Amish. By many people's standards, they would be considered fanatical."

"Fanatical by Amish standards?"

"I didn't know John." Hannah stood and grabbed a few napkins from the holder and offered them to Emma and Sarah at the nearby table. Emma had a big glob of sprinkles stuck to her cheek. Sarah ate her ice cream neatly with her spoon, watching a boy on a skateboard jump the curb. "Is the ice cream good?" Hannah asked, forcing a smile that didn't reach her eyes.

Emma's eyes grew wide, and she nodded. Sarah smiled tightly. "Thank you, Sheriff Maxwell."

"You're welcome."

Spencer thought he noticed Hannah shiver.

Spencer reached out and touched her hand. "You okay?"

"Not really." She ran a hand across her brow. "Not long ago, I was thinking maybe it was time to get a haircut, maybe paint my nails pink. Now I'm wearing my dead sister's Amish gown and making plans for her daughters."

SIX

Later that afternoon, Hannah got Emma and Sarah settled in with a book so she could meet the tow truck driver from AAA out by the barn. Spencer was supposed to arrive soon and install the locks on the doors. She was looking forward to the distractions because she had just called her supervisor at the bank and resigned her position. Her mouth had been so dry she wasn't sure she was going to get out the words. But she had. And it was done. She was still wavering about her long-term plans, but she couldn't abandon the girls now. And her job wouldn't keep.

Hannah gathered her skirt in her hand and crossed the yard to meet the tow truck driver who'd just arrived. The cab of his white truck had the letters *Apple Creek Towing* with a little Amish buggy on the side. She smiled at the irony of it. She figured it was all in the marketing.

The tow truck driver hopped out of the cab, a perplexed look on his face. Hannah forced a smile and shook her head. "It's a long story." She handed him her AAA membership card and smiled at him. While he was calling in her information, she grabbed her cell phone and charger from the car. She'd have to figure out another plan for charging it in the near future. The driver finished his call and connected her vehicle with chains and hoisted it up on the flatbed truck. When he was finished, she asked him to drop the car off at Al's Garage in town. Al was going to put on four new tires and nearly drain her savings. Such was the life of a single, bank-teller-turned-Amish mom. She hoped to sell the car and use the money to hold her over. That was, if there was money left over after she paid off her loan.

"Okay, ma'am." He tipped his baseball cap at her. He hesitated before getting back into the cab. "If you don't mind me asking, I thought your people didn't drive cars."

Hannah gave him a weary smile. "We don't." She lifted her hand in a wave. "Al's expecting my car. Thank you."

The driver gave her a sheepish nod and climbed into the truck. She stood in the driveway and watched as the truck bobbled over the wagon-wheel ruts. *Well, there goes another piece of my past.*

A rustling sounded from inside the barn. Narrowing her gaze, Hannah moved toward it. Another nudge of guilt pinged her insides. She had pretty much left Samuel to take care of the animals the past few days. Her sister wouldn't have been so lax.

The thought of her sister's body in the silo forced her to catch her breath. *Poor Ruthie.* Would Hannah ever be able to fill her sister's shoes?

Once she reached the doorway of the barn, she noticed a dusting of hay sprinkling down from the loft like snow. Perhaps a bird of some kind had found its way into the loft.

Then she heard it. A trill from a cell phone. From the hayloft. Her heartbeat kicked up a notch.

"Hello?" She stepped back and stretched onto her tiptoes to try to see into the loft, but she couldn't. The ringing stopped almost as soon as it started. "Who's up there?" she asked when no one answered.

More hay sprinkled down from the loft. Then the top half of a head with thick brown hair peered over the edge of the loft. Samuel, her farm hand and Willard's son. "It's me, Miss Hannah."

Hannah let out a relieved breath and pressed a hand to her chest. "What are you doing up there?"

He disappeared and for a minute, Hannah thought he was going to ignore her question. "Samuel Fisher, come down her this instant."

"Coming, Miss Hannah. I just have to…"

"Bring whatever it is you had with you down here." Hannah stood with her hands on her hips as the boy backed down the ladder, a burlap bag flung over his shoulder. When he reached the ground, he turned and strode toward the door, a determined expression on his face.

"Wait a minute." Hannah's pulse thumped in her ears. "What were you doing up there? Was that a cell phone I heard?"

Samuel looked down and dragged the toe of his boot across the hay. "I…um…I…" His cheeks grew bright red.

"Tell me right now, or I'll be forced to address this matter with your father." There was no way Samuel knew she was bluffing.

A scared expression haunted the teenager's eyes. "Oh, please don't. He'll be mad. He won't understand."

Sympathy blossomed in her chest, but she had to remain strong. "I'm not mad. I want to know what you were doing in the loft. You don't have any business up there at this time of day, do you?"

"*Neh*, ma'am."

"Then tell me."

Samuel yanked at the edge of his burlap bag and pulled out a book. It looked like a science-fiction title. Surprised, Hannah tipped her head and studied his face. "You were reading up there?"

The boy nodded. "My *dat* thinks it's a waste of time. He thinks I need to direct all my focus on farming." Samuel shrugged, making himself seem so much younger than his seventeen years. "Taking care of God's land."

"And you have a cell phone?"

Samuel nodded. "Some of *die Youngie* have cell phones. It's frowned upon, but it's overlooked during *Rumspringa*. A bunch of us got them at the superstore in the next town. I have enough odd jobs to pay for it." He dropped the book into the bag and twisted the burlap opening, a nervous gesture. "My *dat* wouldn't understand."

"I know all about struggling with a parent."

The boy looked up at her, hope glistening in his brown eyes. "Is that why you left the Amish?"

"Did your *mem* share my past with you?" He was way too young to remember the scandal when a young Amish girl named Hannah Wittmer jumped the fence.

"I overheard *Mem* and *Dat* talking about it."

"*Mem*? Rebecca, your stepmom?"

"She is my *mem* now." He fingered the strap of his burlap bag.

"What did you overhear?"

"*Mem* and you were good friends, and *Dat* thinks it's best if you didn't rekindle your friendship." The color rose in his cheeks, as if he realized he had said too much. "I don't mean to be rude, but I have to get home. *Dat* will be looking for me."

"I've had a few problems around here since my sister died. Do you know anything about that?"

Samuel unwound the bag. "What problems?" He poked at the hay with the toe of his boot. He had a tendency to do that.

She jerked her thumb toward the open barn door.

"Someone slashed the tires on my car. Someone may have knocked over a lamp causing a small fire in the barn."

The boy shook his head, fear evident in his eyes. "*Neh*, it wasn't me."

"Have you brought any of your friends around here? Perhaps you mentioned that you were helping me out?"

"I didn't." Samuel shifted his feet. The set of his mouth was hard to read.

Hannah held up her hand. "You can go, Samuel."

"Are you going to tell my *dat*?"

"No, unless you think I have reason to."

He shook his head. "I'll be back in the morning to take care of the animals."

"Sounds good." Hannah watched as Samuel took a few steps toward the door. "Oh, and Samuel, you're welcome to read your book here anytime. Just knock on the door of the house and let me know you're here." She had gotten lost in the hayloft more than once herself as a young girl while reading Laura Ingalls Wilder.

An I-can't-believe-my-luck smile played across his lips. "Thanks, Miss Hannah."

"And one last thing."

"Yes?" Samuel's whole demeanor had brightened.

"If you ever need anything, just ask. I'm a pretty good ear."

Samuel lowered his gaze without saying anything.

"Have a good afternoon."

Samuel nodded and spun around. He broke into a jog, but the fear on his face when she mentioned telling his father was etched in her memory. What was the boy so afraid of?

"This isn't exactly in my job description." Spencer turned the last screw into the plate of the dead bolt on Hannah's front door. Locks had been installed on all the doors, including her mother's.

"Thank you." Hannah handed him a cold glass of lemonade.

Hannah sat on the rocker on the porch and gently rocked back and forth, pushing off the floor with her bare foot. A chip of pink nail polish clung to her big toenail.

"It's peaceful out here." Spencer placed the screwdriver into the toolbox and snapped the box shut. He crouched down and examined his work. Installing the locks had taken less time than he had anticipated.

"I suppose if I'm going to raise these girls, I need to expand my circle of friends. Make it a little less quiet for the girls. The neighbors came by with food after my sister died, but their visits stopped long before the last casserole was consumed."

Spencer glanced around. "Are the girls still at your mother's house?"

"She likes the company. She's all alone with her thoughts." Hannah looked off in the distance, squinting against the sun low on the horizon. "That's what I miss about the outside world, all the distractions. Radio, TV, computer, you name it. A person can get lost for hours without once examining their thoughts."

"Do you think that's a good thing?"

"Sometimes I'd love to get lost in a game of Angry Birds."

Spencer tested the lock one last time and sat on the rocker next to Hannah. "Really? You don't strike me as an Angry Birds kind of person."

She laughed. "That game's addictive. Have you played it?" She stopped suddenly and looked at him. "Tell me something about you."

Spencer chuckled, surprised by the abrupt change of topics. "Didn't we already cover that topic? Change of pace. Small-town life appealed to me."

"I can't imagine a guy like you didn't leave someone brokenhearted back in Buffalo." Her cheeks flushed pink.

Spencer scrubbed a hand across his close-cropped hair. "Actually, someone I cared about broke my heart. Turns out her idea of a husband was a corporate lawyer, not a city cop."

Hannah stopped rocking. "Oh, I'm sorry. I didn't mean to pry. I was trying to be funny…"

Spencer nudged her bare foot with the tip of his boot. "And what pretty feet you have."

Hannah tipped her head, and he was left to

inspect the top of her white bonnet. He reached out and traced the edge of her cap where it met her soft brown hair. Hannah lifted her head, and he dropped his hand. He couldn't quite read the expression on her face. Alarm? Annoyance? Horror?

Clearing his throat, he held up two shiny gold keys on a small wire loop. He knew he should apologize for being so bold, but he wasn't sorry. This young woman fascinated him, even if he had no business being fascinated by her. He had fallen for the wrong woman before. But Vicki and Hannah were different extremes. Vicki was about money and success. Hannah was...well, Hannah.

Spencer dropped the keys into her palm. "The keys are identical. Each works on the front and back doors. One key opens both the lock in the handle and the dead bolt. I left the key for the lock on your mother's door on her kitchen table."

Hannah closed her fingers around the keys. "Thank you. I'll sleep better tonight." She rearranged her dress over her legs. "I've been thinking about why John might be coming around to harass me."

Spencer studied her closely. "We don't know for sure it's him."

Hannah's lips twitched, as if she were holding back her emotions. "Hear me out. John's not in his right mind. Maybe he found out Ruthie was meeting with me. Maybe that's why he killed her. If he couldn't control her..." All the color drained from her already pale skin. "I blame myself. If she hadn't been meeting with me…"

Spencer reached out and touched her knee briefly. "The only one to blame for your sister's death is the person who—" he lowered his voice because it seemed to be the respectful thing to do "—who ended your sister's life. Don't you dare blame yourself."

Don't blame yourself?

How many times had his friends tried to convince *him* of that? Yet he did blame himself. If he had kept a closer eye on Daniel in Buffalo, the boy wouldn't have been murdered on a street corner.

"Hey…" Hannah's soft voice cut through his reverie. "Where did you go just now?"

"Nowhere. Just tired."

The look of skepticism in her eyes told him she wasn't buying it.

"I get it. I'm tired, too." She leaned back and rested her head on the back of the rocker.

Spencer gathered her hands into his. "You don't have to stay here. I can take you and the girls someplace safer."

She pulled her hands away. "No. I can't do that to Emma and Sarah or my mother." She uncurled her fingers and looked down at the keys for the newly installed locks. "We'll be safe."

He couldn't resist covering her hand again, dragging his thumb across the smooth skin on the back of her hand. "I'll make sure you and the girls are safe."

Hannah bowed her head and covered his hand with hers. "Why is it I finally meet a great guy now?"

Spencer couldn't stifle his smile. "You think I'm a great guy?"

Shaking her head, she leaned back and sat very still. "I'm embarrassed." She pushed to her feet and scooted past him. She braced her hands on the porch railing, her back to him

Spencer joined her. "I didn't mean to embarrass you."

She ripped her bonnet from her head. She smoothed a hand across the flyaways and tugged at the bun a bit, but left it in place. "When I was in Buffalo, the few relationships I had with guys ended because they thought I was too conservative." Hannah flicked him a sideways glance. "They made me feel so...awkward." She brushed her pinky against his on the railing. "You've always made me feel comfortable."

"I feel a but coming on..."

Hannah turned to him and gave him a sad smile.

"I'm trying to be a good parent to my nieces. And if that means being Amish, then so be it. And that means you can't keep hanging around."

Disappointment twisted his insides like a kick to the gut.

"My faith is important to me. I don't want to

put words in your mouth, but I get a sense—" she searched his eyes for a moment "—I sense you lost your faith somewhere along the way."

Feeling exposed, Spencer turned away. God had let young Daniel down and in turn, Spencer *had* lost faith. But something about this woman and her devotion to doing what's right sparked the kindling to his renewed faith. Just maybe...

"I think we met for a reason," Hannah continued. "God wanted our paths to cross. Perhaps so you could be our protector." She ran the flat of her hand across the railing. "We live in different worlds." Hannah nodded slowly as if she had convinced herself of something.

Oh, if only circumstances could have been different.

He leaned in close and tipped her chin, forcing her to look at him. "Just because you're chasing me away, doesn't mean I'm not going to do my job. I'm the sheriff, and my job is to keep you safe."

Indecision darkened her eyes. He hoped maybe this meant he had a chance. Then his heart plummeted. How fair was that? The only way they could have a future was if she left the Amish once and for all. He learned a long time ago, you couldn't force someone to live a life they hadn't signed up for.

Vicki's harsh words scraped across his memory.

Cold, icy regret settled in his gut. He had a job to do. That was all.

* * *

Spencer missed seeing Hannah. He had hoped to run into her in town, but either he had the worst timing, or she hadn't been off the farm much since he last saw her several days ago.

Spencer's police cruiser found its way out to the Lapp farm. Something he did several times a shift while he was on patrol. The late-afternoon sun burned bright in the sky on the sweltering summer day.

Near the Lapp farm, a young man in a buggy tipped his hat at him as his horse galloped down the street. Spencer knew he wasn't the most welcomed guy in the Amish community, but if he could prove to them that he was on their side, he'd hoped to win them over. The Amish wanted to live apart, but sometimes the two worlds collided. And when a law was broken, Spencer knew they'd need him.

The Amish couldn't live completely separate.

Spencer parked and walked up to the house. He heard soft singing coming from inside. *Hannah.* He hated to knock, knowing it would halt her singing. He waited for a moment, listening, and laughed when he recognized the Top 40 pop tune. It wasn't a song the young Amish would sing at their Sunday gatherings.

He knocked and as expected, the singing ceased. Hannah appeared at the door, drying her hands on a dish towel.

"Didn't mean to interrupt," Spencer said through the screen door, trying to subdue his smile.

"Oh, I didn't see you come up the driveway." Almost reflexively, she lifted her hand to her bonnet. Hannah glanced out the door and around him, a shy smile growing on her pretty lips.

"It's just me. Were you expecting someone?"

"No." She took a step back, yet seemed reluctant to invite him in.

"Is something wrong?" He flashed his best disarming smile. He knew exactly what was wrong. He wasn't holding up his side of the bargain to stay away. Let her settle into her new Amish life.

She mirrored his smile and dropped her shoulders. "Please come in. I was about to check on the girls. They've been playing outside, and I need to take the laundry off the line."

He detected a hint of fatigue in her tone. "Your job is never done."

"You're telling me." She lowered her voice. "I miss the days of a nine-to-five job and popping in a microwave dinner then plopping in front of the television. I didn't realize how good I had it." Then just like that, her cheeks turned pink, and she lifted her hands to them. "Listen to me. I'm being selfish…"

"You don't have to explain anything to me." He leaned in close and whispered, "I won't tell anyone."

Hannah glanced toward the kitchen. "I better go check on the little ones. Last I saw them, they were playing on the back porch. They promised me they'd be good." She rolled her eyes as if she wasn't sure she should believe them. "They've been fascinated with a stray cat they found yesterday."

She walked toward the back door, her bare toes against the hardwood floor. Her long dress flapping against her legs. Despite her Amish wardrobe, she had a modern air about her. Or maybe he thought that because he had caught a glimpse of the woman she was in her jeans, sweatshirt and ponytail.

One can't unsee who a person really was. He rubbed a hand across his jaw and followed her through the house and onto the back porch.

Sarah sat with her legs crossed, petting an orange tabby cat.

"The cat seems to be pretty domesticated. I wonder if someone is looking for it," Hannah said, her tone none too concerned.

"A neighbor's, maybe?" Spencer suggested.

Hannah shrugged, then a line deepened on her forehead. "Where's your little sister?"

Sarah looked up, a look of disinterest on her features. "She liked to help *Mem* with the laundry. I think she's in the yard."

Hannah locked eyes briefly with Spencer before snapping her attention to the yard. A laundry line was stretched between a pole and a tree around the far side of the house. She ran down the steps and around to the side of the house.

A row of dresses of various shades of blue and

purple ended where an out of place sweatshirt, jeans and pj's clung to the line.

"Oh, my…" Hannah ran over to the clothesline. She touched the shredded fabric and turned to meet Spencer's gaze. Her sweatshirt had met a similar fate. All her English clothes had been shredded and splattered with something black.

"Where's Emma?" she asked more urgently, fear straining her features. Sarah had strolled over with the cat in her arms. She shrugged again. Spencer scanned the yard, unease prickling the hairs on the back of his neck. Out of the corner of his eye, he noticed movement near the corner of the house.

Little Emma walked over with her black hands, palms up. "*Mem*'s laundry was never dirty." Her lower lip jutted out in a pout.

Hannah ran over and crouched in front of the child and pulled her into a fierce embrace without regard for her dirty hands. "Are you okay?" She pulled Emma out to arm's length and gave her a once-over. "Are you hurt?"

Emma shook her head. "My hands are sticky."

Spencer crouched next to both Hannah and Emma. "Where did you get your hands dirty?" A pungent odor, like tar, reached his nose.

The little girl pointed to the side of the house. Spencer stood and walked around to where she pointed. Next to the house was a bucket of what looked and smelled like tar. A few sets of footprints were in the muddy yard.

He glanced back at Hannah and the girls, all eyes watching him. "Did either of you see anyone out here?"

Emma glanced over at Sarah, and the two of them quickly shook their heads. Almost too quickly.

"Are you sure you didn't see anything?" Hannah asked.

"No, *Aenti* Hannah," Sarah said. Emma bowed her head and bit her lip.

Sarah buried her face in the cat's fur. Emma inspected her hands.

"Let's get you cleaned up." Hannah guided the child by the shoulder. "Spencer, would you mind watching Sarah until I get back?"

"Of course." He sat on one of the rockers on the back porch and Sarah settled down with the cat. His gaze drifted to the side yard, where the Amish clothes hung clean on the laundry line and Hannah's English clothes fluttered in the wind, tattered and stained. Destroyed.

SEVEN

Hannah grabbed the laundry basket and slipped outside to take her destroyed clothes off the line. Tears burned the backs of her eyes as she stretched to pinch the clothespins. Her favorite pair of jeans dropped into her arms.

She tapped her index finger gingerly over the black, tacky tar. She had purchased these jeans after she had saved enough money from her job as a bank teller. She sighed heavily, her lungs filling with the nasty scent of tar.

The designer jeans had symbolized her first success of sorts. She had, for the first time, felt like an official *Englischer*. She was proud of herself, a feeling so foreign to her Amish roots.

An emptiness expanded in her chest. She'd never be able to afford to replace them.

You don't need to replace them.

Hannah worried her bottom lip and dropped the jeans into the laundry basket.

"Are you okay, *Aenti* Hannah?" Hannah spun

around to find Emma staring up at her. "Are you sad because that man ruined your fancy clothes?"

"Did you see who did this?" Hannah struggled to keep the panic out of her voice.

Emma glanced down and played with the folds of her dress. "Um…"

Hannah knelt in front of her niece and forced a smile, even as her pulse whooshed in her ears. "It's okay. You can tell me."

Emma shrugged her thin shoulders. "I saw Samuel."

Hannah swallowed hard, and her ears burned hot. "You saw Samuel do this? Samuel, who helps around the farm?"

Emma nodded, her eyes wide.

"When did you see him?"

"A little while ago."

Hannah smoothed a hand over the cotton of her cap. "Did you see him throw this yucky tar on my clean laundry?"

Emma shook her head slowly. "No. He was running. Fast."

"Which way did he run?"

Hannah spun around to find Spencer standing behind her. She guessed he had heard the entire conversation.

"That way." Emma pointed toward the road, toward the Fisher's house.

"We should go talk to him," Hannah said then hesitated. "But I'm not sure it's a good idea to talk to him in front of his father. When I talked to him earlier, he seemed afraid of his father."

"I'll talk to him." Spencer crossed his arms over his broad chest, anger tightening his mouth.

Hannah grabbed his arm. "No. The sheriff showing up will only make matters worse." A band of indecision tightened around her chest and made it hard to breathe. "I need to talk to him."

"I'm not letting you go alone." The determination in his eyes left no room for debate.

Hannah patted Emma's shoulder. "Want to visit Granny for a little bit while Sheriff Maxwell and I run an errand?"

Emma's eyes brightened. The child was so eager. A ray of sunshine.

Hannah held out her hand. "Let's get your sister and go see Granny."

After Hannah and Spencer got the girls settled, they took the short drive down the street. Spencer pulled up in front of Willard and Rebecca's house. He reached to open the door, and Hannah grabbed his arm. "Wait. We need to talk to Samuel without his father. You wait here. I'll knock on the door, pretend I need to talk to Samuel about his chores on the farm."

Spencer gave her a brief nod, indecision flickering in his eyes. "Okay. I'll be right here, watching."

Hannah mimicked his quick nod and pushed open the car door. She strode up the porch, her laced boots heavy on the wood planks. She closed her eyes and said a silent prayer that she'd know what to say if Willard answered the door. Lying wasn't in her makeup, but a little white one was warranted under the circumstance, if it meant protecting Samuel. She didn't want to accuse him of anything in case Emma was mistaken.

And if Samuel was pulling these destructive pranks in some misguided attempt to chase her away, she needed to get through to him. Yet she didn't want him to run away from Apple Creek if his stern father came down too hard on him.

Like she had run away from her stern father.

Hannah pressed her fingers to her temples. A headache threatened behind her eyes.

Rebecca appeared in the doorway with that wary expression she had come to wear. Hannah missed her bubbly friend. So much had changed since their youth. Rebecca angled her head to look around Hannah to the police cruiser parked on the street.

After a long hesitation, Rebecca pushed open the door, the dish towel pressed to her chest. "Is something wrong? Is Samuel…?"

Hannah took her friend's cool hand in hers. "No one is hurt." She lowered her voice. "I was hoping to talk to Samuel. Isn't he here?"

Rebecca narrowed her gaze. "I'm not sure where he is. I expected he'd be home for dinner by now."

"Is your husband home?"

"Willard's out in the barn." She lowered the dish

towel to her side. Worry lined the corners of her eyes. "Do you want me to get him?"

"I'd like to talk to you alone first, if I may."

All the color drained from Rebecca's face. "I don't know…"

"You can have friends, right? I'm dressed appropriately." Hannah cocked her head and smiled. "We're friends. Remember?"

Rebecca shrugged. "I can talk for a minute. Out here on the porch."

Hannah nodded, studying her friend's face. "Is Samuel having trouble at home?"

Rebecca's expression grew shuttered. "Samuel's a *gut* boy."

Hannah weighed how much she should say. She didn't want to cause any more trouble for Samuel, but if he had destroyed her clothes on the wash line, he needed help. And he needed to be stopped.

"Can I share something with you, and can you promise me you won't get mad at Samuel?"

Rebecca's long pause gave Hannah all the permission she needed.

"I found Samuel in my barn reading a book his father wouldn't approve of." Hannah decided to ease into the conversation.

Rebecca's forehead twitched, but she immediately smoothed out her expression. The dish towel she twisted in her hands received the brunt of her emotions.

Hannah touched her friend's forearm. "It wasn't

anything horrible. He was reading a novel that seems to be very popular today. I read it myself. Other than some fantasy themes that you might not like, it's rather a good book."

Rebecca's expression grew pinched, and her gaze flicked to the doorway.

"He was afraid his father wouldn't approve."

"No, Willard wouldn't," Rebecca muttered. "He likes to limit what Samuel reads." Her knuckles turned white around the twisted dish towel. "I'll make sure I tell Samuel to stick to his chore list when he comes over."

"No, that's not why I stopped by. I felt bad for him. I struggled myself when I was his age."

Anger flashed in her friend's eyes. "Don't fill his head with ideas." She pointed adamantly to the ground. "Samuel belongs here in Apple Creek. With his family. He is my son. Don't…" Her voice wavered.

"I would never do that, Rebecca. I'm worried. If Samuel is afraid of his father, he might run away on his own. You don't want to lose him forever."

Rebecca met her friend's gaze and hiked her chin. "What did you need to speak to my son about? This book? I will talk to him about it." Something flitted across her dark eyes that unnerved Hannah.

"There's something else." Hannah watched Rebecca's face on the verge of crumbling. "Someone threw tar on my English clothes. I want to know if Samuel knows anything about it." Hannah made a spontaneous decision not to tell her friend that Emma had seen Samuel running away from her farm.

Rebecca's brow furrowed. "Of course he doesn't know anything about it. He's a *gut* boy." She started waving the dish towel at Hannah like she was a housefly she needed to shoo away from her freshly baked pies.

"Rebecca!" Willard's voice boomed from inside the house. He must have come in through the back door. Rebecca flinched, and Hannah immediately regretted any trouble her presence might cause her friend. Footsteps sounded through the house, and then Willard appeared at the screen door.

"I didn't realize we had company." Willard stepped outside, his gaze searing the length of Hannah before he turned his focus to Spencer's cruiser parked on the road. "Is something wrong?"

Hannah took a step back. "Spencer...Sheriff Maxwell stopped by the farm, and when I needed to talk to Samuel he offered to drive me over."

"You need to talk to Samuel? He's not home. Can I help you with something?"

"She wants Samuel to come fifteen minutes earlier in the morning because she has a few extra chores," Rebecca interrupted. "I told her that would be okay as long as he was home in time to do chores around here."

Willard studied his wife. He opened his mouth to

say something then stopped. He nodded. "Samuel will come by earlier in the morning. Anything else?"

Hannah shook her head, feeling foolish. She waved and turned on her heel. *"Denki."* She hustled down the stairs toward Spencer, who had gotten out of the car. She caught his elbow and turned him around.

Spencer opened the door for her, and she climbed in. Her gaze drifted to the porch where Willard watched her. Spencer got in his side and slammed the door.

Her stomach dropped. "I'm worried Willard overheard Rebecca and me. I had no intention of getting Samuel into trouble with his father."

"Even if he destroyed your property?"

"What if Emma was mistaken? She's only a child. What if it was John as we've suspected all along? Maybe Samuel had witnessed something and ran away." A weight pressed heavily on Hannah's lungs. "And if Samuel did destroy my clothes, he's a troubled young man. I fear Willard's temper would only strike fear and resentment in his son and make Samuel lash out more."

After Hannah put her nieces to bed, she grabbed a plastic garbage bag and slipped outside to the back porch to where her ruined clothes sat in a laundry basket. She picked up her jeans and muttered, "Some nerve."

"We'll catch him."

Hannah spun around, her hand pressed to her beating chest. "You scared me." She had to stifle the urge to slug Spencer. The slow smile spreading across his face didn't help.

"Sorry," he said, his voice husky. "You left your cell phone charging in my car." He placed her phone and charger on the window ledge.

"Thanks."

"And I thought you could use some company."

"Hmm…" She was too much in a funk to admit that yes, she was happy for the company. "Keep hanging around here and people are going to talk."

"People talk anyway." Mischief danced in his eyes, which were partially shadowed by the gathering dusk.

She ignored his comment. With swift jerky motions, she stuffed the ruined clothes into the garbage bag. She dropped the bag, and it landed with a plop on the pine planks of the porch. Hannah leaned against the railing and tugged off her bonnet. Her tight bun was giving her a tension headache.

Hannah rolled her shoulders and sighed. "I don't believe Samuel did this."

Spencer sniffed. "Even though Emma saw him running across the yard?"

"Even though Emma saw him running across the yard." Hannah bit the inside of her lip. "He might have been running so I wouldn't see him coming out of the barn again. He's afraid his father will scold him for reading inappropriate books, or using a cell phone." She shrugged, considering another less likely scenario. "Or he might have seen who really ruined my clothes and ran away in fear."

Spencer made a sound from the back of his throat. "I tried to track Samuel down after I dropped you off. No luck. I'll try again tomorrow."

"Yeah," Hannah said resigned. "I suppose we won't know more until we talk to him."

Leaning over the laundry basket, she grabbed her favorite pj bottoms, now pink with splatters of black tar. "You'd think a girl could wear whatever she wanted to bed without being harassed."

She dropped the pj bottoms into the garbage bag and wiped a splotch of black tar from her thumb onto the plastic. "Someone's determined to chase me away."

"Who has the most to gain if you leave?" Spencer's voice was calm, calculating as he was working the pieces of the case. She didn't understand the empty disappointment that suddenly expanded within her. She lowered her gaze, pretending to study the black plastic bag at her feet. This *was* just another case to him. It wasn't personal.

"Lester and Fannie Mae are determined to raise the children," Spencer added, still deep in thought. "And more important, if I leave, they can finally take over the land. They want to farm the land that is sitting idle."

Spencer let out a heavy sigh in the gathering darkness. He stood and joined her next to the railing.

Hannah closed her eyes briefly. "I didn't like Lester from the minute I met him, but would he really be this...underhanded? This destructive? I don't know him well enough."

"I'm going to ask you again, Hannah. Would you please consider leaving the farm with the girls? It would be safer." The concern in Spencer's voice made a tingling start in her fingers and shoot up her arms.

"I can't leave with the girls. Their grandparents and aunt and uncle will argue the case that John will come back. He is still their rightful guardian."

She shook her head. How had she gotten into this mess?

"What's going on in your head?"

"This whole situation is so far out of my element. But there's one thing I learned all the years of living alone in Buffalo." She braced her hands on the railing and hung her head.

"Care to share?" The breeze kicked up. The overpowering smell of tar was replaced by grass and dirt and hay.

"It's cliché but true. The grass isn't always greener on the other side."

"You're telling me." Spencer turned and rested his hip on the railing.

"You?" She angled her head. "You wear your

police uniform very well." She couldn't imagine him not being able to find his place in the world.

Spencer held out his hand and laughed. "You wear your Amish wardrobe with flair."

Hannah smiled demurely. "Flair. Hardly." She swept her hand across her long gown. "I feel like I've been asked to put on clothes that I never thought I'd have to wear again. But I need to search for happiness in here." She covered her heart with her hand. "I was miserable and terribly lonely in Buffalo. I never seemed to fit in. I refused to come back because I had made a mess of things when I left. Now—" she twisted her lips "—maybe this was all God's plans. Allowing me to return. With grace. And to do what my sister would have wanted me to do."

"I wish I had your faith."

Hannah studied his face closely. "Didn't you grow up going to church?"

Spencer frowned. "Oh, we went to church, all right. Sat in the front row. My mother forced us to go."

Hannah's heart sank.

"Once they left the sanctuary, my father went back on patrol, disillusioned with the things he saw every day on the streets. And my mother's only concern was praying my dad came home every night. She was the devout one." He drew in a deep breath and let it out slowly. "My father struggled with his faith. I suppose that's why I've struggled with mine. My father warned me not to become a police officer. He said the job stole part of his soul. I only understood that after I worked the streets of Buffalo."

Hannah covered his hand. "It's never too late…"

Spencer cocked his head and pulled his hand away. He pointed to the garbage bag. "Now about those clothes."

Hannah studied him for a moment. Now was not the time to push issues of faith. She cleared her throat. "Someone wanted to make a point." She nudged the bag with the toe of her boot. "Point taken. I want it to end here. I don't want any more trouble."

"It needs to be investigated. Someone was on your farm. Destroyed your property."

"I know." Her words came out clipped. Tired. "We need to be careful how we proceed. I don't want to get Samuel caught up in this if he's innocent."

"What if he's not innocent?" Spencer seemed to stare right through her, and a bundle of nerves tangled inside her.

A creak sounded by the door, and Hannah spun around. She saw a flash of blond hair before it disappeared. "One of the girls is looking for me. I better go in."

Spencer nodded and strolled down the steps. "Night."

"Night." Hannah slipped inside and closed the

door and turned the key in the lock, something she had never imagined doing as a young girl growing up on the farm. She moved to the window and watched Spencer's shadow disappear around the side of the house as he headed to his car.

Hannah found Sarah curled up in the rocker with the cat in her lap. The creature had made himself completely at home.

"Maybe the cat prefers to stay outdoors. We could make her a soft bed in the barn," Hannah suggested. Growing up, her family had never kept pets in the house. Cats were meant for chasing mice in the barn.

Sarah glared right through her aunt without saying anything.

"Come on." Hannah tapped her niece's shoulder. "It's time to get into bed." She strode toward the stairs, hoping her niece would follow.

"He's not a nice man."

Hannah turned around slowly to see Sarah stroking the kitten's head and staring at her. The girl's eyes were hardened and too cold for the sweet child her sister had raised.

Hannah checked her tone and carefully chose her words. "Sheriff Maxwell is a good man. He's helped me a few times since I returned to Apple Creek." She softened her tone. "And remember he got us ice cream?"

Sarah pinched her lips and shook her head. "*Dat* told me policemen are bad."

Hannah swallowed back her protest. Despite how much she despised John Lapp for what she suspected he had done to her sister, she had to remember he was the girl's father.

"*Dat* wouldn't want him coming around here. When my *dat* gets back, he's going to be really mad."

Anger grew in Hannah's belly, but compassion ruled her brain.

"We need to consider each person for who they are, not their profession. Just because Sheriff Maxwell wears a uniform, doesn't make him bad. In the English world, people count on law enforcement to help them. Even though the Amish like to keep separate, law enforcement is also there to protect us."

"He's nosy." Sarah dragged her hand down the cat's tail.

Hannah sat in the rocker next to her niece and leaned forward, resting her elbows on her thighs. "According to your *dat*?"

Sarah nodded, some of the anger slipping away from her tight expression, perhaps at the mention of her father.

"Do you know why your *dat* would say that?" Hannah trod carefully, not wanting to upset the child. Her mother had died less than two weeks ago and her father had disappeared.

"*Dat* said Sheriff Maxwell knew nothing about the Amish way, and he should keep his nose out of our business."

Replaying her niece's words in her head, Hannah reached over and petted the cat. "Have you named him?"

Sarah's steely gaze faltered. "Pumpkin."

"That sounds like a lovely name."

Sarah scrunched up her face as if she were giving it some thought.

"Why didn't your father like the police? Did something happen?" Hannah was thinking about the fight John got into with his brother in town.

Sarah stroked the cat from head to tail and then again. Without looking up, she said, "My *dat* and Uncle Lester were talking really loud in town." *The fight.*

"Do you know why they were talking really loud?"

"Uncle Lester was mad at *Dat. Dat* claimed Uncle Lester didn't know how important it was to be Amish. My uncle laughed. He thought my *dat* should be farming, not working for someone else."

"Did you hear anything else?" Hannah kept stroking the cat, hoping to keep her niece talking.

"*Dat* said he'd never sell Uncle Lester the land." Sarah's thin shoulders crept up to her ears. "I don't know what he meant."

Hannah tucked a long blond hair behind Sarah's ear. Too much adult stuff for such a little peanut. Hannah leaned in close. "Do you like living here?"

Sarah looked up with a question in her eyes. "*Dat* should be home soon."

Tingles bit at Hannah's fingers and raced up her arms. What if her father was already home? Harassing *her*?

Sheriff Maxwell swung by the police station after stopping by the farm. He had let the pretty Miss Wittmer distract him long enough.

"You're here late." Deputy Sheriff Mark Reynolds sat at his desk with photos spread out in front of him.

Spencer leaned over and picked up a photo. It was of an Amish man with a fat lip, but more important, his beard was slashed at an angle. Spencer slowly lifted his eyes to meet Mark's. "Is this recent?"

Mark let out a long breath. "Yeah, the hospital called." Mark consulted the file in front of him. "Abram Leising was attacked while he slept last night. His beard was cut."

"Last night?" Spencer picked up another photo and studied the pained expression on the elderly man's face.

"Mr. Leising arrived at the hospital late this afternoon. The staff told me he was an unwilling patient. He's already back home."

"We haven't had a case like this in six months."

Mark nodded. "You think it's our missing guy, John Lapp?"

Spencer rubbed his hand across his jaw. "He

was a person of interest in our last break-in and beard cutting."

"How much priority should we give this? I drove out to the Leising farm, but Abram was pretty tight-lipped."

"Did he see the guy who cut his beard?"

"No, claimed it was dark. When he woke up, the intruder punched him in the mouth, dazed him." Mark pushed the photos around with the eraser of a pencil. "I get the impression he wouldn't have come to the hospital except the guy lost a tooth, and his grandson made him come in."

"Maybe it's John…maybe it's a copycat." Spencer mentally ticked through all the events of late. An Amish man's beard was part of his identity. The perpetrator was lashing out against the Amish? Someone who has a grudge against the Amish? Did this sound like John Lapp?

Mark crossed his arms and leaned back in the chair. "How far do you want me to pursue this? The Amish like to live apart from us. Why should this be any different? Let them work it out for themselves. No one's getting hurt…" He hesitated for a fraction. "Not really."

From his perch on the corner of the desk, Spencer assessed his young deputy. "Why don't you tell me how you really feel?"

The deputy slouched, some of the bravado draining out of him. "You don't know what it was like to grow up in this town. The Amish can be a real pain sometimes. They need our help, but then refuse to press charges in court." He waved his hand. "The kidnapping and murder of Mary Miller had the whole town divided. Got my boss fired." He held out his hand. "But I guess that worked in your favor."

Spencer felt a muscle working in his jaw. "It's our job to bridge that gap. Make sure we have a good relationship with the Amish."

Mark stood and strolled toward the door. He turned around and casually crossed his arms. "That may be how things work in the big city, but you can't change people's hearts in a small town. They've already formed their opinions."

"If you really feel that way, you're going to have to look past it to do your job."

Mark slid a hand across his utility belt. "I'll do my job. I always do." He turned to walk away and tossed a "Night, boss" over his shoulder. The word *boss* was edged in a brittle tone.

Spencer dismissed it and glanced down at the photos his deputy had left on the desk. Had John Lapp been responsible for this and previous attacks? Had he been unstable long before he went after his wife? *If* he had gone after his wife…

Guilt wormed its way into his heart. If only Spencer had caught the intruder the first time a church elder was attacked in his home, perhaps he could have prevented Ruth's murder.

* * *

The next morning, Hannah came downstairs in an Amish dress and started a breakfast of eggs and bacon. Any thoughts of resorting to her English wardrobe had gotten tarred and destroyed yesterday on the clothesline, save for a couple pairs of jeans and a few T-shirts. If she could just keep the girls on a regular routine, maybe the rest of the chaos in her life would settle down.

Wishful thinking?

She grabbed the kettle from the stove and went over to the sink to fill it. Through the window, she noticed a dark plume of smoke billowing up over the barn.

Frozen in place, her heart stopped. She spun around when she noticed Sarah's thin coat was missing from the hook. She ran into the sitting room and nearly tripped over Emma, who was stacking blocks in the middle of the floor.

Hannah crouched down and clutched Emma's shoulders, panic making it difficult to talk, to think. "Where's your sister?"

Emma's eyes flared wide. "She told me not to tell you."

Hannah swallowed her growing fear. "You must tell me where she is." She glanced out the window. The sky over the barn had turned black with smoke. "Did Sarah go out to the barn?"

Emma stared at her. Tears filled the little girl's

eyes. It took all Hannah's energy not to shake the information out of her. "Emma, please tell me. Did she go to the barn?"

Hannah stood and ran to look out the window. Red and orange flames licked the roof. "You have to tell me."

Emma nodded. "It's a secret..." The little girl's voice trailed off. Hannah held her breath, waiting for her to reveal what she knew. "Sarah went looking for Pumpkin. She thought you made her sleep in the barn."

Hannah's heart plummeted. "Stay here. Do you understand? Stay here."

Hannah turned off the stove under the bubbling bacon. She grabbed a dish towel and ran it under water. She burst out the back door and bolted toward the barn barefoot. She rolled her ankle on a wagon-wheel rut. Pain shot up her leg, but she ignored it.

"Sarah! Sarah!" she screamed as she made her way to the barn. She scanned the yard. Adrenaline fueled her forward momentum and narrowed her vision.

Dear Lord, please let Sarah be okay. Please let her not be in the barn. Please Lord, let me find her now. Please, please, please...

She reached the barn with no sign of Sarah. The barn door was cracked open about a foot. Enough for a nine-year-old to easily slip through if she was looking for her kitty.

Hannah's stomach revolted.

Not wanting to feed the flames, she squeezed through the door. Black smoke swirled around her. Creaking wood and howling flames sent terror clawing at her heart.

"Sarah!" Smoke gagged her.

Covering her mouth with the damp dishcloth, she pushed forward. What she wouldn't do to not have this full, highly flammable skirt dangling around her legs.

She squinted and pushed farther into the barn. The rough, dry hay felt brittle under her bare feet. Her throat narrowed. *No sign of Sarah.*

In his stall, Buttercup neighed wildly. Holding her breath and covering her mouth, Hannah ran to his stall and opened the gate. The sweet animal was too frightened to move.

Dear Lord, I don't have time for this frightened animal. Let me find Sarah.

She talked calmly to Buttercup and nudged him toward the door. Sensing freedom, he bolted outside to the open field.

Thank you, Lord.

Hannah sucked in a quick breath of fresh air at the door. "Sarah!" she yelled. "Sarah!" She covered her mouth with the damp cloth and slipped deeper into the barn.

Her lungs screamed for air. Stars danced in her

line of vision. She opened the doors at the far end
of the barn and shooed the cow out.

Panic and flames pushed in from all sides.
"Sarah!"

A loud crack sounded. Terror squeezed the
air from her lungs. She glanced up. A shadow
descended on her.

Darkness.

EIGHT

Spencer had pulled onto the road and lifted Mrs. Greene's hot brew to his lips when his cell phone went off. He glanced down and smiled. *Hannah.* Surprised, he lifted the phone to his ear. "Morning."

Silence stretched across the line. His heartbeat kicked up a notch. His intuition told him something was wrong.

"Hannah? Are you there?" He waited what seemed like an eternity until he heard a little voice.

"My *aenti* needs help."

Spencer secured his coffee in the cup holder and pressed the phone tighter to his ear. "Emma?"

He did a quick check of traffic, made a U-turn and pushed the accelerator to the floor in the direction of the Lapps' farm. "What's going on, Emma?"

"There's a fire."

"Where?"

"The barn…" He strained to hear her soft voice above his thrumming heartbeat.

"Listen carefully, Emma. Stay away from the barn. I'm on my way."

"I'm scared."

"It's going to be okay. Where is your aunt?" He held his breath while waiting for the answer.

"The barn."

He swallowed around the lump of terror in his throat. "I'm on my way. Okay?"

Without waiting for an answer he ended the call and dialed dispatch. "Send a fire crew to the Lapp farm on County Route 77."

With his hot coffee roiling in his gut, he gripped the steering wheel tighter.

As he rounded the curve near the farm, he saw bright red flames shooting into the sky backed by ominous black clouds. Adrenaline surged through his veins. He slowed his vehicle and whipped into the driveway. His vehicle bobbed over the ruts in the driveway. He pushed open the door and ran to Emma crouched on the porch, her dress pooled around her legs. She held her faceless doll to her nose. Tears tracked down her cheeks.

Spencer clutched the little girl's arms. "Where's Hannah? Where's Sarah?" His words squeezed out from a too-tight throat.

Emma's watery eyes lifted to the barn.

"In the barn?"

Too frightened, Emma nodded.

"Okay." Spencer watched the black plume of smoke billowing up from the barn. The smell of charred wood made him cough. "Stay right here, Emma. The firemen will be here soon."

Sirens sounded in the distance. Spencer ran to his cruiser and popped the trunk. He grabbed a blanket and raced toward the fire.

A prayer came spontaneously to mind.

Dear Lord, please guide me. Let me find Sarah and Hannah safe.

When he reached the barn, the door yawned open. He pressed the blanket to his face and surged forward, holding his breath. Then his training kicked in. He dropped to all fours where the air wasn't so thick with smoke. He crawled into the barn, the rough feel of hay cutting into his hands.

Fear and panic like he'd never known propelled him forward. He didn't dare yell Sarah or Hannah's name for fear it would be his last breath.

Gloom and darkness pushed in on him from all sides. Heat and panic tightened the collar of his shirt.

Keep moving.

Something, a knowledge, a knowing, made him turn right. Splayed across the barn floor was Hannah. A beam blocked the view of her face. But it had to be Hannah.

He pushed forward and shoved the beam off Hannah's lifeless body. Terror seized his heart.

An image of Daniel flashed in his mind's eye. Too late; he was too late. Again.

He stared, frozen. Every mistake he had ever

made in his past weighed down on him. Would this be the end?

In the flash of a moment, he thought of terrified Emma. Alone with her doll. Mustering a strength he didn't know he had, he drew in a shallow breath near the barn floor. It smelled of hay and charred wood and burning hair.

Spencer slid his hands under Hannah's body, one arm under her legs, the other around her shoulders. He plucked her off the ground and ran toward the exit holding his breath. When he was a safe distance from the barn, he laid Hannah on the grass.

He pushed Hannah's hair away from her face and leaned in close to listen for a breath. Over the roar of the fire and the cacophony of the rescue vehicles, he wondered if he imagined her breath. He pressed his fingers to the pulse point on her neck. *Thank you, Lord.* "Hannah, Hannah." He gently tapped her cheek.

Dear Lord, please let Hannah be okay.

He grabbed her arm and felt her pulse again.

The first hint of relief started pumping through his veins.

"Hannah," he said. "Hannah."

Hannah's eyelids fluttered. Hope blossomed in his chest.

A sputtering cough erupted from her throat. Spencer wrapped his arm around her shoulder and eased her to a seated position. Tears tracked down her dirty cheeks as she coughed and sucked in huge gulps of fresh air.

A firefighter ran to their side with his emergency kit. "Anyone else inside?"

Hannah's eyes grew wide. She struggled to stand, but Spencer made her stay on the ground. "You need to stay put."

"Sarah." She coughed again. "I can't find Sarah."

Hannah couldn't catch a breath. She coughed until tears streamed down her cheeks. Struggling against Spencer's firm hold, she tried to stand. She had to find Sarah.

The heat from the burning barn singed her cheeks. "I can't find Sarah." She covered her mouth with her hands, and grief nearly cut off what little breath she could draw into her lungs. "Sarah, she's nine…" She clawed at the firefighter's turnout gear. "You have to find her. She went into the barn looking for her cat. Please…"

The firefighter pulled away from her and patted Spencer on the shoulder. "Move her back." Then to Hannah, "We'll find your little girl."

"Please…"

The firefighter ran over to the other firefighters and gave them instructions she couldn't hear. But based on his urgent gesturing, it must have been that a child was trapped in the barn.

Spencer's hand felt heavy on her back. She

wanted to fling it away and run into the barn herself. Find Sarah.

She'd die if something happened to Sarah. She had promised Ruthie she'd make sure her children were safe. An image of little Emma popped into her brain.

"Where's Emma?"

"She's fine." Spencer's voice was calm despite the chaos swirling around them. He pointed beyond the fire truck. A young female firefighter was crouched next to Emma. It looked like she was introducing a teddy bear to her doll.

A fist of grief tightened Hannah's throat. *"Mem..."*

"She's okay, too."

Hannah's gaze drifted to her mother standing in her doorway, clutching something to her chest.

Hannah bowed her head, feeling the weight of the world on her shoulders. She had let her sister down.

She had let poor, sweet Sarah down.

A firefighter came back over to them. He opened a huge medical kit, much like the toolbox her father used to have. "Ma'am, I'd like to look at that head injury."

Absentmindedly, Hannah touched her forehead and pulled her hand away. Blood and soot marred her fingertips. "I'm fine."

Oh, she was far from fine. She lifted her arm;

the effort sent a sharp pain through her upper arm. "Find my niece. Please. I'm fine."

The firefighter made eye contact with Spencer, who nodded. The firefighter walked away, but left his kit next to them.

Hannah struggled to her feet with Spencer's help. "I have to do something. I can't just stand here. Sarah's—" An explosive cracking sound filled the air. The roof of the barn collapsed into itself. A spray of sparks filled the air.

Terror pumped through her veins. Sarah had been her responsibility. Hers...

She pressed her palms together and touched her lips. *Please, Lord, bring Sarah safely back to me.*

The firefighters aimed their hoses at the fire. She turned toward Spencer, who gathered her into an embrace. She pulled away from him.

"Walk around that side of the barn."

Spencer narrowed his gaze at her.

"Please, I'll go around the other way. I have to do something."

Hannah strode around the barn. The acrid smell of burning wood filled her lungs. "Sarah!" she screamed. "Sarah!"

A quiet whimper caught her attention. She slowed her pace. The heat from the barn only ten feet away warmed her face. She stopped and strained her ears against the roaring fire, the fire hoses and the shouting of the firefighters.

"Sarah!"

Another whimper.

Hannah spun around and faced the trees. She ran to the edge. The fallen branches scraped her bare feet, her bare legs.

Hannah cupped her hands and shouted her niece's name again. She squinted into the dark shadows. Suddenly, a darker shadow rushed at her from the trees.

Sarah!

The child flung herself at Hannah, wrapping her arm around her waist and burying her head into her side. Tears blurred Hannah's vision as she smoothed the little girl's hair. She bent over and kissed Sarah's forehead. She smelled of fire and earth. And heaven. Pumpkin meowed in Sarah's other arm.

"Oh, sweetie," Hannah said into Sarah's hair, "are you okay?"

Sarah nodded.

A firm hand touched her shoulder. Hannah glanced up, and Spencer smiled down on her. "Is she okay?" he asked, his voice gruff.

"I think so."

Hannah reluctantly pried the little girl's arm from her waist and crouched to look at her. Flames danced in her terrified eyes. "I—" the little girl swallowed hard, her gaze drifting to the fire "—I wanted to see Pumpkin. I figured you made her go stay in the barn."

Hannah cupped Sarah's cheek. "Oh, sweetie. I

didn't. She must have gotten out herself somehow. Did you go in the barn when it was on fire?" Scolding her now seemed ridiculous when everyone's emotions were running high.

Sarah shook her head. "The barn wasn't on fire. I found Pumpkin next to a hay bale. I started to get her when I heard a man yelling. Pumpkin ran past me and into the woods." She stroked the kitten's head. "I had to find her."

"You heard a man yelling?" Spencer asked.

Sarah nodded again.

"Did you see him?"

"No," Sarah said in a very soft voice. Her lips quivered.

Hannah rubbed her hand up and down her arm. "Did you hear what the man said?"

"He said, 'Get.'" Spencer and Hannah locked gazes. Tingles of fear rained down on her like hot sparks from the fire.

"Is that all?" Hannah forced a smile, trying to draw the child out.

"I don't know…" Sarah whispered. Hannah smoothed her hand over her niece's soft hair in much the same way as Sarah stroked her beloved kitten's head.

"It's okay, honey. It's okay."

Spencer wrapped his arm around Hannah's shoulder, and the three of them walked to the other side of the barn. Her mother stood on her porch with Emma.

Emma broke free and bolted toward them, her little arms pumping, a huge smile on her face. "You found Pumpkin!" Emma shoved her new bear in her big sister's face. "And I got a new toy."

Hannah cupped Emma's chin. Complete peace settled around her. She lifted up a silent prayer.

Thank you, Lord, for keeping my family safe.

The next morning, Spencer yawned and squinted against the rising sun as he drove out to check on Hannah. He grabbed his travel coffee mug from the cup holder and took a big swig. He was going to have to hook up an IV of caffeine to stay awake today.

Yesterday, once the fire was contained, Hannah had insisted she was fine and that Spencer leave.

He had questioned the neighbors, including the Fishers. No one had seen anything. Young Samuel claimed he had finished his chores and returned home before the fire started. He hadn't seen anything out of the ordinary and no, he hadn't seen Sarah out looking for her cat.

Twenty-four hours later, he had no evidence to prove differently.

When Spencer reached the farm, two buggies sat in the driveway. Apparently, word had gotten out about the barn fire. He stepped out of his pickup and strolled over to join Lester, the bishop, Willard and his son, Samuel. A regular party. But no sign of Hannah.

They were talking excitedly and pointing to the barn. They were probably planning a barn raising. He had watched the Amish with fascination gather for a weekend and construct a barn. Old-fashioned techniques did not mean inefficient.

"Officer Maxwell." Willard seemed to take in Spencer's casual clothes. "Any word on what caused this fire?"

Spencer crossed his arms and widened his stance. There was something about this guy that rubbed him the wrong way.

"It's still under investigation."

Willard lifted a skeptical eyebrow. "And you're working on your day off?"

Spencer didn't like the implication in his question, but he let it go.

Willard placed his hand on his son's shoulder. "My son here saw something yesterday, and it's best if he tells you all at the same time."

Lester adjusted his hat back on his head and Bishop Lapp made a *hmm* sound.

Spencer's pulse whooshed in his ears. He shifted his gaze to Samuel. "Why didn't you tell me you saw something when I questioned you yesterday?"

Samuel kicked a clump of mud with his boot and shrugged. He cut a sideways glance to his father.

"The boy was afraid. That's all." Willard's authoritative tone left no room for discussion. "He's here now."

Samuel looked up, a hint of something indiscernible in his eyes. "I saw someone running out of the barn."

Spencer narrowed his gaze. He locked eyes with Willard then glanced back to his son.

"Go on." Willard nudged his son with his elbow. A flash of annoyance, and then fear crossed Samuel's features. The boy was seventeen, on the cusp of being a man. His father wasn't going to be able to bully him for much longer.

Samuel cleared his throat and looked Spencer in the eye. "I had finished cleaning Buttercup's stall when I heard heavy footsteps, too heavy to be Miss Wittmer's or one of the little girls…" Samuel seemed agitated as he plucked at his suspenders.

"I ducked behind some hay bales when I saw Mr. Lapp."

"Mr. Lapp?" An uneasy feeling settled in Spencer's gut.

"John Lapp," Willard added.

"You saw my son?" The pain and confusion in Bishop Lapp's tone was palpable.

"My boy," Willard continued, "saw John Lapp march into his very own barn with a canister of gasoline. Only through *Gott*'s good will did my son escape."

"Are you saying Mr. Lapp started the fire and then ran out?" Spencer studied Samuel's face. Red blossomed on his cheeks. Willard never removed his hand from his son's shoulder.

Bishop Lapp bowed his head, his expression hidden by the broad brim of his hat.

"Why would my brother do such a thing?" Lester stepped closer to Samuel. "You have to be mistaken."

Samuel toed the hard-packed earth, freeing another clump of dirt. "He didn't see me. I ducked to the side and then when the flames started coming, I ran home."

"Why didn't you alert Hannah?" A mix of anger and disbelief hollowed out Spencer's gut.

Samuel swallowed hard. "*Yeh*, well, I was afraid. I heard the rumors…that he killed Mrs. Lapp. I wanted to get away. Far away."

Willard clapped his son's shoulder. "You did *gut*."

Lester let out a heavy sigh and ran his hand down his scraggly beard. A look of capitulation crossed the hard angles of his features. "I suppose John has been struggling. Only *Gott* knows what's in his heart. I fear I don't know my brother anymore."

"My son is alive." Bishop Lapp's shaky voice was almost inaudible, but Spencer caught the trace of hope in it. "John is alive."

Lester's brow furrowed. "*Dat*, this is not good news. John burned down his barn."

"My boy saw what he saw," Willard interrupted.

"My younger brother…" Lester pushed back his straw hat and shifted his feet, effectively blocking out Willard. The men obviously did not like each other.

"Would you like to talk in private?" Spencer offered.

Lester hesitated a minute. "*Neh*. My feelings in this community are no secret." He tugged on the brim of his hat. "My brother was not content to follow the *Ordnung*. He questioned the rules and our father all the time. My father is not a young man. He should have been respected. The rules of the *Ordnung* are agreed upon by the community. Yet John kept wanting to push his will on all of us."

"Were his ideas radical?" Spencer studied Samuel, who seemed fidgety.

"They were what you might call extreme," Lester said, somewhat apologetically. "He wanted the Amish of Apple Creek to stay separate from the rest of the world."

"I'm confused," Spencer said. "Aren't the Amish already separate?"

"We set ourselves apart. We are to follow Romans 12:2." Willard squared his shoulders and continued. "'Do not conform any longer to the pattern of this world, but be transformed by the renewing of your mind.'"

Lester held up his hand. "The sheriff didn't come here for us to preach at him. We all know how you feel about the Amish ways, Willard. If you and my brother had your way, we wouldn't interact at all with the English."

A muscle ticked in Willard's jaw. "The outside world is an evil place. We must protect our ways."

"We are both conservative and practical," Lester said, purposely not looking at Willard. "We know we can't completely isolate ourselves. We adapt as the world moves around us."

Willard seemed unusually quiet.

"What do you think, Mr. Fisher?"

"John and I were friends. But John deviated from the path. He lost his way." Willard shook his head in obvious disgust, then he clapped his son on the shoulder. "Unless you need anything else from us, we have chores to do." He turned to Lester. "Let us know how we can help your family rebuild here."

Willard and Samuel climbed into their wagon and left.

"Mr. Lapp, you and your family need to be cautious until we take your brother into custody."

"I'd feel better if my nieces weren't staying here. My wife and I could keep them safe at our home now that it's obvious my brother is never going to be able to care for those girls."

"Sarah and Emma have their aunt." Spencer glanced toward the house. Still no sign of Hannah.

Shaking his head, Lester pursed his lips. "Those girls need to be in a stable family. With a proper *mem* and *dat*." He lifted his palm to the burned out remains of the barn. "Sarah could have been killed in that fire.

"I'm going to take the girls today. They've experienced enough tragedy in their short lives. The girls need to be raised in a proper Amish family." Lester fingered his beard.

"Perhaps the family can have a meeting and come to some sort of agreement." Spencer knew Hannah wasn't going to hand over her nieces.

"I will not agree to let my nieces stay under Miss Wittmer's care." Lester made a sound of disbelief.

The screen door creaked open, drawing Spencer, Lester and the bishop's attention. Hannah stepped onto the porch wearing jeans and a T-shirt. Her long brown hair flowed over her shoulders. She strode over to them, a determined look in her eyes.

"I'm done. I can't live like this anymore."

Hannah pushed open the door and stepped onto the porch. As if she had yelled, "Look at me," all eyes landed on her. But the face she focused on belonged to Sheriff Spencer Maxwell.

Why did she care so much about what he thought?

She pushed back her shoulders and a twinge of pain shot down her arm. Dismissing it, she strode across the yard, careful not to twist her ankle on one of the ruts. Her head pounded with each step. She planted her hands on her hips, trying to muster a confidence she didn't feel. "I'm done. I can't live like this anymore."

She ignored the smug look on Lester's face and instead focused on the hurt expression on Spencer's. "Can I talk to you in private?" she asked, trying to quell the tremble in her voice.

"Where are the girls? Fannie Mae and I will take them home right away."

Closing her eyes briefly, Hannah took a calming breath. "The girls are with their grandmother."

Lester strode toward the *dawdy haus*. Hannah ran after him and grabbed his arm. He stopped and looked down at her, then at her offending hand. She let go, but said in no uncertain terms, "Leave the girls, please. Give me a few minutes to talk to Spencer, then I'll explain everything."

Indecisiveness crossed Lester's face. He didn't say anything, but he didn't move, either.

Hannah held up her hand. "Give me a minute to talk to Spencer." She was surprised her words sounded so calm despite her dry mouth, her racing heart.

Lester cleared his throat. "I'm going to take some measurements." He turned on his heel and walked toward the barn.

Hannah was too focused on her decision to register Lester's comment.

"Can I talk to you…on the porch?" Without waiting for an answer, Hannah stuffed her hands in her jeans pockets and walked toward the porch and hoped Spencer would follow. The calmness that had settled over her in the middle of the night—when she had made her decision to leave the farm—took flight and was replaced by a million butterflies flitting in her stomach. She hadn't planned on making the announcement to Lester and Bishop Lapp this soon.

She reached the porch and grabbed the railing. She lowered herself onto the second step, fearing her knees were going to give out.

Spencer sat next to her and patted her knee. "What's going on?"

Her gaze drifted to the burned-out barn. Willard had come by this morning with Samuel and had taken the animals over to his farm to care for them until her barn was rebuilt. She was sure she could talk Rebecca into keeping them long-term, unless… Her gaze drifted to Lester measuring up the barn.

Her focus faded. "I'm leaving the farm."

From the look on his face, Spencer seemed to be struggling with something. "You're going to let Fannie Mae and Lester raise the girls?"

Horror shot through her. "Oh, no. Absolutely not. I promised my sister I'd make sure they were taken care of. It was only after the fire that I realized I could take care of the girls much better if I…if I was living on my own terms."

"You've thought this through."

Hannah bowed her head and threaded her fingers through her hair. Had she thought this through? Or had she made a knee-jerk reaction to a near-death experience?

"Maybe it's for the best." Spencer gave her a boost of confidence.

"You're probably the only one who will agree."

Spencer shifted to look at her. Something in his expression made her blood pressure spike. "What is it?"

Spencer told her what Samuel had witnessed right before the fire. Hannah muttered, "I can't believe it…"

"I've notified dispatch. All patrols will keep an eye out for John."

Hannah pushed to her feet and swiped a hand across the seat of her pants. "Is that apartment in your building still available?"

"I'll call Mrs. Greene, my landlady."

"Thank you." She wrapped her hand around the railing. "I have to talk to my mother and the girls now."

Would she be able to talk her mother into moving with her?

Lester and Fannie Mae came to mind. If her mother wouldn't leave her residence, maybe she could get Lester to move into his brother's house. They could come to some agreement. They'd be close if her mother needed anything. And Hannah would still be in Apple Creek. They might treat her like an outsider, but there was no reason she had to be shunned.

Unease tickled the far reaches of her mind. Fannie Mae and Lester had always wanted the land to farm, didn't they? And Hannah was about to give them exactly what they wanted.

NINE

Instead of dragging the girls out of the only home they've ever known the exact day Hannah made her announcement, she decided to ease the girls into the transition. Now, a few days after she dropped the bomb in *typical* Hannah fashion—if she were to take Lester's mumblings to heart—she was still living in her sister's home. But not for long.

Hannah glanced out the window. She caught the tail end of a horse and buggy as it trotted down the street. She had a few more things she wanted to clean and tidy before Spencer arrived to drive them into town. His landlady, Mrs. Greene, was more than willing to rent the fully furnished apartment on a month-to-month basis.

Upstairs, Hannah found Emma stuffing her face-less doll into a suitcase Spencer had dropped off. Sarah sat stone-faced on the bed with her arms crossed over her middle. Hannah suspected she'd have to pack a few things for the older child.

Emma glanced up and smiled. "Do you think

we could get one of those pretty dolls you mentioned? I'd like the dolly *Mem* made for me to have a friend."

"We'll have to buy a lot of things at first. Once we get settled, we can look into another doll." Thankfully, her car sold so she'd have a little extra money, but she'd have to be careful until she found a job. The apartment was located in the center of town, so she should be able to walk for necessities.

"Dolls are stupid." Sarah's harsh words snapped Hannah out of her musings.

"Sarah!" Hannah said, unable to keep the shock from her voice. *Lord, give me patience*, Hannah had prayed more than once.

She opened her mouth to offer some encouraging advice to her sullen preteen when she heard the door creak downstairs. She held up a finger. "Pack your things. We're moving to the apartment this afternoon. I don't want to keep Sheriff Maxwell waiting."

Sarah huffed.

"I know this is difficult, but things will get better. I promise." Hannah hustled down the stairs. She came up short in the kitchen when she found her mother sitting at the kitchen table. *"Mem."* She immediately ran a hand down her T-shirt and jeans.

"You're leaving today?" Her mother's voice had a faraway quality.

"I've delayed long enough." She pulled out the

chair and sat across from her mother, guilt pinging her insides. "I'm worried about you out here."

Her mother waved a shaky hand in dismissal. "*Yah*, well. We've been over that. I must live in the Amish community."

Hannah had tried every argument to convince her mother to live with them in the apartment. But her mother was unwilling to walk away from her Amish faith, and that's what she was convinced she'd be doing if she left her home.

Hannah was deeply frustrated, sad, but she understood. Her mother was a humble Amish woman.

"Well…Rebecca's nearby if you need anything. And soon Lester and Fannie will be living in Ruthie's house."

The lines deepened around her mother's mouth. "I suppose it will be *gut* to have someone farming the land again."

"I'll work with a lawyer to make sure Lester pays you a fair price for the land."

"*Gott* will see me through."

"I'll only be a few miles away." The words did nothing to ease the guilt weighing heavily on her.

"You'll be further away in your heart." Her mother's gaze was unwavering.

"I want you to see your granddaughters as much as possible. I hope we can do that."

Her mother studied the table. She ran her gnarled hand along its edge. "It seems like only yesterday I was feeding you and your sister at this table."

Her mother drew in a deep breath, filling her lungs. Hannah stopped and watched her mother, a million conflicting emotions tugging at her heart. "*Mem*, I'm sorry I couldn't stay. I tried..." Her words rang hollow. How hard had she tried? She had only been here for a couple weeks.

But the fire. The fire had cemented her decision. A decision she had struggled with from the minute she slipped on her sister's black Amish dress and tried to pick up Ruthie's life where she had left off.

She couldn't do it. She had to live her life as best she could given she now had two little girls who were counting on her.

Her mother reached out and pulled her hand into hers, something very uncharacteristic for her mother. "You were never happy here."

Time seemed to slow around them. *"Mem..."*

Her mother shook her head. "Your father was hard on you. Harder than he ever was on my Ruthie..."

A flush of warmth rolled over her. Something about the way her mother said *my Ruthie* made her both sad and jealous.

Hannah was about to protest when her mother squeezed her hand and said, "When I was eighteen, I left Apple Creek...I was a lot like you." She lifted her watery eyes.

A lump formed in Hannah's throat. Her mother had left Apple Creek?

"I met a nice man. An *Englischer*." Her lips flattened into a thin line. "I thought we were going to be married."

Hannah listened, fascinated, her heartbeat pulsing in her ears. She had never known this part of her mother's life.

Her mother's gaze dropped to the scarred pine table. "I got pregnant."

Hannah stifled a gasp, one of surprise, not of disapproval. The last thing she wanted was for her mother to think she disapproved or was being judgmental.

Emma ran into the kitchen, her loud footsteps snapping Hannah out of her intense focus.

"Sarah said she's staying here, but I want to go with you." The determined set of Emma's jaw reminded Hannah of Ruthie.

Hannah ran her shaky fingers over her niece's silky hair. The little girl had grown fond of leaving her hair down.

Eager to continue the conversation with her mother, Hannah swallowed hard. "Go upstairs with your sister. Tell her I'll be up in a minute to talk. Okay? Look around and make sure you have everything you might need. Hairbrush, your doll..." She'd have to buy new clothes for the girls once they started their new life, but for now, they had to gather what they could.

Emma nodded and spun around, the skirt of her dress flaring out. She watched her niece run away and thump up the stairs. Muffled complaints floated down the stairs.

Hannah shifted to face her mother and covered her mother's hands. "What happened?"

"We were supposed to get married. We were making plans. He was hit while riding his bike to class at the university…" Her mother got a faraway look, and she shook her head.

A ticking began in Hannah's head. A warm flush of realization washed over her. She swallowed around a knot of emotion. "I'm that baby."

Her mother set her jaw and closed her eyes briefly, her shame so deep she couldn't say the words.

Hannah jerked back and pulled her hands down into her lap. In one instant, she had learned her father wasn't her father, and her real father was dead. She blinked back dizziness.

Her mother folded her hands in front of her and hiked her chin. "I came back to Apple Creek, heartbroken. Ashamed."

Hannah fought back the tears. She wanted to ask her mother a million questions but feared she'd stop sharing altogether.

"I married Eli Wittmer, a good Amish man. He had always been sweet on me before I got worldly ideas." She sniffed and closed her eyes. "He accepted the child I was carrying as his own. No one knew any differently."

Her mother closed her eyes and nodded. "Your

father, the man who raised you, saved me from shame. He allowed me to be a respectable Amish woman."

Mesmerized by the in and out of her own breaths, Hannah reframed her entire life. It made sense, explaining why the only father she had known favored Ruthie, his true daughter, while coming down hard on her.

"Eli was a good man, but he looked at you and remembered what I had done." Her mother unthreaded her fingers and threaded them again. "I'm sorry. It wasn't your fault."

The walls pulsed, and a bead of sweat rolled down Hannah's back. "*Mem*, why are you telling me this now?"

Her mother's lips pursed then relaxed. "You need to follow your heart. You were never happy here. Go. I know Ruthie would want you to raise her daughters, even if it's not on this farm in the Amish community."

She squeezed her mother's hand. A tear trailed down Hannah's cheek, but she didn't bother to wipe it away. The information her mother had shared, although difficult for both of them, had been an amazing gift.

"Lester and Fannie Mae are going to fight me for the girls."

"Do what you have to do to keep them." Her mother put her palms on the table and stood. She cupped Hannah's cheek. "I was happy raising my family here, in the Amish community. But I can see in your eyes, this life is not for you." She coughed and put her fisted hand to her mouth. "Just promise me a few things."

Hannah waited.

"Make sure you visit me often. I can't bear to lose you and your sister *and* my granddaughters."

"Of course. I'm not leaving Apple Creek."

Her mother gave her a knowing look. "Oh, I fear you will. But wherever you go, make sure you keep *Gott* in your life. In all of your lives."

Hannah swiped a hand across her wet cheek. "I will, *Mem*. I will..."

"But why can't I keep the cat?" Sarah whined from the backseat of Spencer's truck. She had Pumpkin curled up in her lap. His heart went out to the little girl.

Hannah shifted in her seat, her features strained. "Sweetie, the apartment doesn't allow us to have animals. My friend Rebecca said she'd take good care of Pumpkin."

"What if she runs away? She ran away before."

Spencer cut a sideways glance to Hannah. She blinked slowly a few times, as if giving it some thought...or praying for strength. "Pumpkin found her way to us, right? God was looking out for her. We fed her and made sure she had someplace safe to sleep. She's a smart cat. She'll be fine."

In the rearview mirror, Spencer watched Sarah smoothing her hand down the kitten's head and back.

"God will make sure Pumpkin is cared for," Hannah reassured the child.

"Maybe God wants *us* to protect Pumpkin."

Hannah slumped into the seat and tugged on the seat belt, defeated.

When Spencer pulled in front of the Fishers' property, Sarah instinctively tucked Pumpkin under her chin.

"Come on, you can show Pumpkin her new home," Hannah said, forcing a cheery tone.

They all climbed out and headed toward the barn in back. "We can say hello to Buttercup, too," Hannah added. Rebecca's family had taken in all their animals displaced by the barn fire. Although tragic, the barn fire and the subsequent removal of the animals from the farm had allowed Hannah to make the choice to leave. A part of Spencer felt hopeful this meant a possible future for them.

Spencer resisted the urge to reach out and place a reassuring hand on Hannah's back. She looked as if she was ready to bolt, as if she expected Willard to storm out of the house and demand she get off his property now that she had fully embraced her English roots.

The door creaked open, and Rebecca hustled

toward them, a look of worry on her face. "Samuel is gone. I've checked everywhere, and he's gone!"

Hannah clutched her friend's arm. "What do you mean?"

"He must not have come home last night." Her eyes blazed with fear.

"I'll have patrols keep an eye out for him, but boys his age do that on occasion."

"Oh, I don't know. Willard wouldn't like law enforcement to get involved."

"He doesn't have to know," Spencer reassured her.

"I shouldn't go against my husband. He's out looking for him." Rebecca dipped her head. "At least we know he's not hiding in your barn. The fire took care of that." Resentment or something else flattened Rebecca's lips into a thin line.

"I never encouraged him to hang out in my barn to read." Hannah's tone was rightfully defensive.

"Perhaps you didn't discourage him enough."

Hannah opened her mouth then snapped it shut.

Spencer brushed his hand briefly across Hannah's back, a silent show of support.

"Why do you think he left?" Spencer considered a few scenarios. Could he have been responsible—perhaps accidentally—for the barn fire and run away in guilt? Perhaps he had lied about seeing John Lapp there to protect himself.

"Samuel's been hanging around the wrong people," Rebecca said quietly. "The stricter his father got with Samuel, the more he rebelled." She kept cutting her gaze toward the barn. When Willard strolled out, Spencer understood why.

"We came to drop off the cat," Hannah said.

Willard's hard gaze shifted to the cat in Sarah's arms. "Go on and put it down, child. That cat'll be fine. We'll see that it's fed. And we'll have a few less field mice around here for our troubles." He let out a gruff laugh.

Sarah buried her face in the kitten's fur before setting the cat down on the ground. If only Mrs. Greene wasn't allergic.

Willard cleared his throat. "My wife is sharing news of my Samuel. He'll be fine. He's doing what some young Amish boys do. He'll come home once he gets it out of his system. I did. He'll realize worldly ways are not for him."

Willard scrubbed a hand across his unkempt beard. "Now, about Sarah and Emma…"

Hannah reached out and clutched Emma's hand, tugging her closer. Sarah stood with her chin pressed to her chest, watching Pumpkin explore the long grass near the edge of the barn.

"The girls and I will be fine. Thank you for caring for the animals." Hannah seemed to be measuring each word. "Come on girls, let's go."

"There are plenty of Amish families that would willingly take in Sarah and Emma Lapp."

"They are my nieces." Hannah turned and strode toward the truck.

Emma skipped next to her, holding her hand, oblivious to the tension hanging in the air. Sarah followed, begrudgingly, unwilling to leave Pumpkin behind.

"They are meant to be raised Amish," Willard called out as Spencer helped the girls get into the truck. He opened the door for Hannah.

Spencer slammed the door. "Hannah will make sure her nieces are well cared for." He narrowed his gaze, cautioning Willard to back off, as he walked around to the driver's side.

Once inside the truck, Spencer turned to Hannah. "What do you make of Samuel taking off?"

"I'm not sure. He's afraid of Willard."

"Hmm…I remember being afraid of my father when I was a kid. I did some boneheaded things when I was young, and I knew my father was going to make sure I stayed on the straight and narrow." Spencer turned the key in the ignition. "That's what happens when your father's a cop. He understood what was at stake if I screwed up."

"My father was strict with me." There was a faraway quality to her voice. "And I ran away."

"That makes three of us." He thought of the girlfriend and law practice he had left behind. He tipped his head and unsuccessfully tried to coax a smile out of her.

"I fear there's a big difference here. Samuel has

been at the center of some suspicious activities. Do you think this makes him look guilty?"

Spencer slipped the gear into Drive. "It doesn't scream innocent."

Emma sat on her new bed in the apartment and bounced. "I have my own bed? I don't have to share with my sister?" The awe and sincere excitement in her young niece's voice warmed Hannah's heart after a rough couple of weeks.

"You should find everything you need to get settled." Mrs. Greene ran her hand down the hand-stitched quilt, probably made by one of the Amish women looking to earn extra money. The irony wasn't lost on Hannah.

"Thank you so much, Mrs. Greene. I appreciate your letting us move in so quickly."

Mrs. Greene waved in dismissal. "It was sitting empty. And I like having it occupied. I don't feel quite so alone. Sheriff Maxwell has been busy lately and hasn't had time for our evening chats." Her blue eyes twinkled. "I guess now I understand where he's been."

Hannah opened her mouth to protest and settled on a smile instead.

Mrs. Greene walked toward the bedroom door and patted the door frame. "I'm right downstairs if you need anything."

"Thank you." Hannah turned to her older niece. "Do you think you'll like it here, Sarah?"

Sarah stuffed a dress into the drawer, shoved it closed with her hip and narrowed her eyes at her watchful aunt.

Hannah slipped out of the bedroom, letting the girls get used to their new surroundings. She found Spencer unloading groceries in the kitchen. "Thank you."

He turned around, a warm smile on his handsome face. "It's the least I can do."

Hannah slumped into the kitchen chair and rested her chin on the heel of her hand. "Do you think I'm doing the right thing?" Her head was swirling with all the changes.

With news of her biological father.

But she couldn't share any of that with Spencer for fear of betraying her mother. It was a heavy burden to bear.

Spencer placed the instant coffee on the shelf in the pantry and turned to face her. "You've made a lot of tough decisions in your life."

"Like leaving the Amish for the first time?"

He nodded. "That had to be the toughest decision."

She rubbed her forearms. "This is harder because now I'm making decisions for my nieces." She glanced toward the bedroom to make sure they couldn't hear them talk. "Emma seems up for the adventure. But I'm afraid Sarah will never forgive me. She thinks I'm going against everything her parents raised her to believe."

Wasn't she?

She looked up and found Spencer watching her, a look in his eyes that she couldn't quite define.

"How can I make such a huge decision for them? What if I'm wrong? What if they end up—" she shook her head "—I don't know on drugs or…"

Spencer slipped into the chair across from hers and covered her hand. "No parent knows for sure they're making the right decision. You'll have to have faith, right?"

A smile tugged on the corners of her mouth. "I'm surprised to hear you talking about faith." She narrowed her gaze. "Or are you humoring me?"

"I'm here for you. For whatever you need." They locked gazes. He leaned across the table, and her heartbeat kicked up a notch. He leaned and brushed his lips against hers. Warmth coiled around her heart.

She pulled back and pressed her fingers to her mouth.

A half smile quirked his lips. "I'm sorry."

She shook her head slowly. "No, don't be sorry." A new feeling, hope maybe, made her smile. "The kiss was nice, but I have so many things going on right now. I can't think straight."

Spencer pushed away from the table and stood. He brushed his hand across her shoulder. "I have to go, but you know how to reach me."

"Thank you." She had been saying that a lot lately. She sighed heavily and listened to his footsteps retreat across the hall to his apartment. From the girls' bedroom she heard arguing. Her shoulders slumped, and all the energy and determination that had driven her to march out of her sister's home in jeans and a T-shirt evaporated.

Since Hannah had sold her car, she was glad the apartment she rented was within walking distance from town.

In usual fashion, Emma skipped alongside Hannah and chatted while Sarah was her moody self. Hannah felt a little guilty for not giving the poor girl more slack, but Hannah was doing everything she could think of to bring the nine-year-old around. When they reached the thrift shop, Hannah decided to look for clothes for Emma first, hoping Sarah would eventually warm up to the idea.

Hannah pulled out a few pretty tops and khaki pants for Emma. The little girl grabbed them excitedly. She was extra excited when her aunt added a bright pink skirt, so different than the plain clothes she was accustomed to.

As expected, Sarah was much harder to please. Everything she touched was in dull blues and browns. Hannah pulled out a bright purple skirt and a white blouse with blue and purple flowers on the collar. It wasn't exactly what nine-year-olds in the city would wear, but it seemed to be a nice compromise—a transition between her Amish clothes and the English world she was being forced to enter.

Hannah watched Sarah's tentative expression as she fingered the flowers on the collar. A faraway look descended into her eyes. After a moment, she looked up. "*Mem* liked pink roses." Her face grew flushed and her eyes shiny. "I miss *Mem*."

Hannah's heart crumbled. Deep inside this petulant child was a little girl who missed her mother. Holding back tears, Hannah reached out and pulled Sarah into an embrace. "I miss her, too." Hannah traced Sarah's long braid with a finger. "I know this is hard for you. I promised your mom I'd make sure you were well taken care of, and this is the only way I know how."

Sarah buried her head into Hannah's side and nodded.

"I wasn't very good out on the farm."

"We'll do much better in town. And we'll be close to Granny and your other family."

Sarah stepped back and held the skirt. "I like this one. Do you think I could get some of those shoes I saw over there?"

Hope blossomed in Hannah's chest. "Show me."

The three of them wound their way around the racks of clothes to a display of colorful sneakers."

"Of course." Hannah playfully tugged on a strand of Emma's hair. "Let's try on a pair for you, too."

Ten minutes later, they walked out of the store, the girls dressed in their new English clothes.

Emma fit in quite nicely in her purple sweatpants and T-shirt with a kitty on it. Sarah looked cute, but a little dated in her long skirt and Peter-Pan-collar blouse.

Small steps.

Her heart burst with joy and hope.

A police cruiser pulled up alongside the curb, and Hannah squinted against the sun reflecting off the windshield. The door swung open, and Spencer climbed out. The serious expression on his face made her good mood evaporate. Something was wrong. Definitely wrong.

Hannah leaned over and said to the girls, "Go look at the cute things in that window." Emma ran ahead to peer into the boutique window. "Go on now." Hannah nudged Sarah when the girl didn't move. After the second prompt, Sarah did as she was told.

"What's wrong?" Hannah asked Spencer.

Spencer took off his hat and sunglasses. She didn't want to explore the look in his eyes. She wanted to hold on to the feeling of hope she had only moments ago.

"Is it my mother?" Terror seized her heart. She should have never left her mother alone on the farm. She should have forced her to come to the apartment with her.

"No," Spencer said, "it's John Lapp."

"You arrested him?" Panic seized her heart. Her eyes drifted to her nieces. *He's going to claim he's innocent, and he's going to fight for custody of the girls.* The girls she was finally winning over.

"It's not what you think."

Hannah pressed a hand to her heart. The world narrowed to a small tunnel. "What happened?"

"Hikers found John Lapp's body in the woods. It looks like he killed himself."

Her heart dropped. She looked over at the girls. Emma was pointing out a stuffed kitten in the window to her sister. Sarah was only half paying attention, seemingly more interested in her and Spencer, but she was too far away to hear them.

Panic heated her cheeks. *Oh, what was she going to tell sweet Emma and Sarah?*

Another piece of her heart shattered for her nieces.

Emma and Sarah's father was dead. There would be no goodbyes. No tearful jailhouse visits.

Nothing.

Her brother-in-law had taken the coward's way out. He had killed himself. She plucked her T-shirt away from her heated skin. She couldn't think straight through the haze of anger.

"We'll never know what happened or why—" she lowered her voice even more "—with Ruthie."

Spencer cleared his throat. "John Lapp left a note."

Hannah's heart stuttered. *A note?*

Spencer seemed to be watching her warily, as if he feared she was going to pass out on the sidewalk.

He touched her arm lightly. "It would be best if you and the girls came down to the station."

"Oh, okay." Hannah forced the words out. She didn't know how much more the girls could take.

A quiet calm descended over her.

Maybe with John gone, they could finally get on with their lives.

Maybe.

TEN

The sheriff's station was surprisingly busy for a small town. Spencer led Hannah and her nieces across the office. Seated in a far corner were Fannie Mae, Lester and Bishop Lapp. Hannah reflexively squeezed her nieces' hands. *She* was going to raise them. She had promised her sister.

"I didn't know everyone was going to be here," Hannah whispered, leaning forward so only Spencer could hear.

"We decided it best if everyone was here when we read John's letter." Spencer glanced down at the girls; a hesitant expression flashed across his face.

"What about Sarah and Emma? They shouldn't be here."

Spencer held out his palm. A young woman dressed in a uniform approached them. "Hello," the officer said, smiling brightly. "I'm Officer Pyne. Perhaps the girls would like to come with me and have some cookies and juice."

Hannah squeezed the girls' hands again. "It's

okay. Go with Officer Pyne. I'll be right over here talking with the grown-ups."

Emma went eagerly, but in usual form, Sarah seemed hesitant. She went along all the same. Hannah stood rooted in place as she watched the girls follow Officer Pyne into an adjacent room Hannah assumed was the break room.

Nerves tangling in her stomach, Hannah joined the small group clustered in a corner lined with uncomfortable-looking beige plastic chairs. Knees going weak, Hannah sat, leaving two open spaces between her and Fannie Mae. The Amish woman shifted her knees toward her husband, who sat on the far side of her as if Hannah had somehow offended her.

"Thank you all for coming here under short notice." Spencer walked around his desk and grabbed a folded piece of paper from the drawer. "I'm sorry for your loss."

John Lapp's father, the bishop, made a sound of discomfort and leaned on his cane heavily as he lowered himself into a chair. "My youngest son lost his way a long time ago."

Lester sat rigid. By his side, Fannie Mae fidgeted with her skirt. "Now that we know John's…" Fannie Mae couldn't get the word *dead* out of her mouth. "Lester and I should take the girls. They belong with us. They need to be raised in an Amish family." She held out her hand. "*She* has them dressed like *Englischers*. Their parents would be so disappointed."

Hannah scooted to the edge of her chair, her heart pounding in her ears. "Now, wait a minute…"

"We have a lot to sort out." Spencer held up his hand. "Let me read the letter John left. It was found next to his body."

Nausea clawed at Hannah's throat. How desperate John must have been to kill her sister and then kill himself. *Lord, give me strength to get through this day.*

The bishop crossed his wrists on his cane and bowed his head, as if bracing himself.

Hannah tucked her hands under her thighs and pulled her arms close to her body. Suddenly, she was very, very cold. The air-conditioning pumping out from the ceiling vent didn't help. She clenched her mouth to keep her teeth from chattering.

Spencer unfolded the letter. "This is a copy of the letter. The original is evidence." He lifted his eyes and locked gazes with Hannah before he started to read.

"Sorry. I hurt many people. I pray Gott forgives me. Sarah and Emma should be raised by my brother Lester Lapp. He and his wife have a gut home."

The chatter in the room swirled around Hannah's head. The voices sounded loud, garbled, unintelligible. The walls closed in on her. The papers on the bulletin board swirled and blended and loomed out, a moving 3-D collage. She blinked. Her palms grew moist. Panic made her want to flee. She closed her eyes and drew in a few deep breaths, trying to tamp down her emotions. She willed herself to focus.

Opening her eyes, she blinked back the sight of Spencer crouched in front of her, a look of concern on his handsome face.

"You okay?"

Hannah blinked a few more times. She looked up to find three more pairs of eyes on her. Lester offered her a cup of water. She took a sip and her light-headedness subsided.

Seeming satisfied that she was fine, Lester said to Spencer, "So, it's settled then. We'll take Emma and Sarah home to live with us."

Alarm swept over Hannah. She jumped to her feet and felt the hard plastic of the chair pressing against the back of her knees. She swallowed hard and prayed for strength. "Nothing is settled. Not if you think you're going to take my nieces from me. My sister—" she lowered her voice for fear the girls might hear "—was killed by your brother. My sister asked that I make sure her children were cared for."

"Ruth would want her children to be raised Amish." Fannie Mae clasped her hands and pressed them to her chest. "You may think I'm stern, but I only want what's best for the girls. I would be a *gut mem*."

For the first time, Hannah noticed a softness, a sincerity, about the woman she had initially overlooked. Hannah bit the inside of her cheek then finally found the words, "I am going to raise the girls."

Lester threw up his hands. "My brother expressed his interests, too. Don't his wishes count?" His question was obviously directed to Spencer. "He specifically documented what he wanted."

"The note is not a legally binding document, if that's what you're asking. We don't even know if he wrote it."

Lester blinked rapidly under the brim of his straw hat. "Who would have written it? Are you suggesting he didn't kill himself?"

Hannah watched Spencer carefully. He kept a neutral expression that did nothing to calm her nerves.

"We have no reason to believe your brother's death is anything more than what it looks like on the surface." Spencer crossed his arms over his broad chest and stepped closer to Hannah. "This letter does not give Lester and Fannie Mae legal custody of Emma and Sarah."

Lester bristled. "We don't have to live within your legal system."

"What can I do, Spencer? Can I file for full custody of the girls now that we know their father isn't coming back?" Hannah hated the desperate tone of her voice.

"This isn't something we can resolve right now. I suggest you allow the girls to stay where they are and maybe the two families can come to some sort of agreement. A judge will have the final say."

The bishop, who had sat quietly all this time, pushed to his feet. "*Neh*, the children cannot spend part of the time in the outside world and the other part as Amish children. It would lead to much confusion."

"I am not going to hand them over." Hannah lifted a shaky hand to push back her hair.

"I did not suggest you turn them over," the bishop said. "I ask that everyone go home and pray. Pray that we make the right decision for these two orphans."

Hannah slowly shifted her attention toward the break room where her nieces were probably drinking soda and having a treat, blissfully unaware. They were the true victims.

A sharp pain jabbed her stomach. How was she going to tell her nieces their father was dead?

Spencer escorted the Lapps to the exit, then returned and found Hannah sitting where he had left her.

He sat. "You okay?"

She nodded but didn't say anything for a long time. When she finally looked up, her eyes shimmered with unshed tears. "John's really gone?"

"Yes."

She nodded again and swiped a tear. "How likely do you think it is that I'll get to keep the girls?"

He searched her eyes. "Is that what you want?"

She rubbed her forehead. "I believe it's best for the girls."

"Then I recommend you go through the legal system. I suspect Lester and Fannie Mae will fight it, but it's the only hope you have."

"Okay, okay…" Hannah seemed to come to some sort of conclusion. She pushed to her feet. "I need to get the girls. Get them home." She sucked in her lips. "I have to tell them about their father."

"I can come with you."

She nodded, a mournful expression on her face.

"Give me five minutes, and I'll take you home."

"I need to pull myself together before I face them."

Spencer squeezed her shoulder in a show of comfort then crossed the office space to a filing unit. His fellow officer, Mark Reynolds, approached. "Looks like you were right all along. That John Lapp was up to no good. He was the one who attacked the church elders and cut their beards in the middle of the night."

"We still have a lot of unanswered questions," Spencer said noncommittally, yanking open a file drawer.

Mark rested his beefy arm on the credenza. "Why defend him? The guy spelled it out in his suicide note. He was mad at the elders for not enforcing stricter rules." Mark rolled his eyes. "Who knew an Amish man would want stricter rules?"

"I didn't share that part of the note with the family."

"You can't tell me a guy who kills his wife and offs himself wasn't the guy who broke into the homes and whacked the beards off some old Amish guys. He was a loose cannon. You called it. Looks like we'll be able to close two cases."

"Show a little respect. We need to give the family time to grieve before we interview them about the beard-slashing case." His fellow officer's lack of sympathy bugged him. "The bishop lost his son."

Mark shrugged. "Do you think Ruth Lapp knew what her husband was up to?"

A familiar guilt nudged Spencer. If he had identified John as the perpetrator earlier, could he have saved Ruthie?

Unable to sleep, Hannah climbed out of bed and checked on Sarah and Emma. The girls both were sound asleep in their twin beds. Blessed sleep. Sarah had the sheet partially over her face, and Emma had her leg flung over the edge. Sleeping as she lived, with complete abandon. The poor sweet girls had been through more than most people had in a lifetime. When Hannah had broken the news of their father's death, Sarah cried quietly, and Emma appeared less affected, plucking at the hem of her doll's plain dress. It was almost as if Emma hadn't expected her father to come back anyway. Or maybe she was too young to fully understand.

Hannah walked through her upstairs apartment

and double-checked the locks on the interior door and windows. She wished she had some sort of definitive answer from Spencer that John had been the one and only bad guy. With him dead, were she and the girls safe? Spencer had cautioned her that they still had to determine a time of death. The adrenaline pulsing through her veins made it difficult to think straight.

Emma had claimed she saw Samuel running away after her clothes were tarred. But that may have been a teen prank or again, maybe Emma was mistaken. Samuel had claimed he saw John and perhaps he had run away in fear.

Hannah plopped down on the couch and pulled back the sheer curtains and stared over the dark yard. She squinted. Was that a shadow lurking beyond the ring of light cast by the lone streetlight? She dropped the curtain and slumped into the couch. She couldn't shake the feeling someone was out there. Watching her apartment. Waiting for her.

You're safe. John's dead.

And Spencer lived right across the hall.

Footsteps sounded in the hallway. She crept to the door and peered through the peephole. Spencer was unlocking his apartment across the hall. Hannah finger-combed her hair and opened the door.

Spencer turned, a tired and surprised look on his face. "It's late."

"I couldn't sleep."

He slipped his hands into his pockets. "You've had a rough few weeks."

"I'm not worried about me." She drew in a breath and let it out. "I'm worried about the girls." She rested her hip against the door frame. "Did you see anyone outside when you were coming in?"

Spencer shook his head. "Was there someone out there?"

Hannah shook her head briskly, immediately doubting herself. "It was probably shadows. I'm on edge."

Spencer put his bag down. "I'll go check it out."

Hannah grabbed his hand as he passed. "No, don't. I'm sure it was nothing."

Spencer lowered his gaze to her hand touching his and smiled. She quickly clasped her hands behind her back.

"Have a seat." Spencer gestured to the top step.

Hannah sat and rested her shoulder against the wall and shifted to face him. He did the same, and their knees brushed. She wished life could be just this simple: two people sitting in the stairwell talking on a quiet summer evening.

"Do you think I'm doing the right thing?" Hannah hated the uncertainty in her voice.

"What does your heart say?"

She lowered her eyes and studied a chip in the pale blue paint near the pine molding on the stairs.

"I can't live as an Amish person. It's not who I am. Not anymore. But what about Sarah and Emma?"

"Do you think they'd be happy with the Lapps?"

Memories of her father's stern rebukes flashed in her mind's eye. With the new information her mother had shared about her real father, Hannah was now reframing her childhood in a new light. It didn't justify her father's angry outbursts, but it explained why he favored Ruthie, his *real* daughter.

"What?" Spencer tapped her leg gently. "You seem a million miles away."

"Searching for happiness is an English convention. The Amish live God-fearing, humble lives. Community centered. What if…" A horrible idea came to mind. What if her bad decisions prevented Sarah and Emma from eternal life in heaven?

No…

That had been a threat the Amish held over the unbaptized to keep them in line, but even humble Amish didn't feel they were guaranteed heaven. It was a hope. And Hannah had hope in her Christian faith even if she decided not to be baptized Amish. Once her life settled down, she'd follow through with joining a local church with her nieces.

She looked up and locked eyes with him. "I believe that as long as you have faith and you're a Christian, and you live a good life, then it's okay." She tipped her head, and her hair fell in a curtain to cover her face. "Then I think about what a crazy world this is, and I wonder if the sheltered life of the Amish would be better for them."

"The world *is* a crazy place. I thought by coming to Apple Creek, I could escape some of the harshness of it." He sniffed and shifted on the stair, leaning his elbows on his knees. "As you know, before coming here, I worked in Buffalo." He turned his face away from her, but the pain was evident in his voice. "Through an outreach group, I befriended a high-risk boy. He was fourteen…"

Was fourteen…

"I thought I was making a difference. But I couldn't save him from the violence of drugs and gangs. He was shot and killed outside a convenience store running an errand for his mom. He was wearing the wrong colors that day, and a rival gang took him out. I should have been able to do more." He turned and looked at her. The pain in his eyes cut her to the core.

"Like what?"

"I had made a few phone calls about getting his family moved to subsidized housing in the suburbs, but I got distracted. Busy with the job."

Hannah's heart broke for him.

"Is that why you left Buffalo?"

"Let's just say I had reached my breaking point." He gave her a sad smile. "My fiancée…well, my ex-fiancée had been on me. We met in law school.

She had dreams of a nice life in the suburbs, big house, kids."

Hannah tipped her head. "What's wrong with that?"

"Nothing. But she didn't count on her lawyer boyfriend going into law enforcement."

"Why did you? I mean, when you could have made more money as a lawyer."

"I wasn't happy practicing law. I wanted to get out there and do something directly to help people. As much as my dad grumbled about his job as a cop, I admired him. I know some lawyers find a way to help people, but I wanted to be a cop since I was a kid. My father pushed me to be a lawyer. Then my girlfriend pushed me to stay a lawyer. When I passed the officer exam and entered the police academy, she thought it was a phase. Our relationship didn't survive my new career."

"I'm sorry."

His smile made her forget her troubles. "I'm not. All our choices send us down a path. The road might be littered with obstacles, but if things came too easily, we might not appreciate them." He lifted an eyebrow. "God has a plan."

"God has a plan," she repeated. "You seem to have had a change of heart yourself." Warmth blossomed in Hannah's heart.

"You've been a positive influence on me. I never

knew someone with such strong faith in times of adversity. You made me reexamine my own faith."

She tilted her head and smiled. "That's probably the nicest thing anyone has ever said to me."

Half of Spencer's mouth quirked into a smile. He leaned in and pressed a warm kiss to her lips. She reached up and cupped his cheek, scratchy from his five o'clock shadow. She pulled back and smiled. "Why does everything have to be so complicated?"

A twinkle lit his eyes in the dim light. "Want the absolute truth?"

Her heart beat loudly in her ears. "Can I handle the truth?" She laughed, an awkward squeak.

"I have never met anyone quite like you, and I need to open my heart to you."

Hannah's mouth went dry.

"I don't want you to be baptized Amish. I don't want you to leave Apple Creek. I want to see if this—" he waved his hand between them "—is going anywhere."

"I…" Hannah couldn't think straight.

Spencer held up his hand. "But in the end, you have to make the best decision for you."

Her heart beat wildly. "And the girls," she whispered.

"And the girls," he repeated, a look of hope in his eyes. "No one can define you. Only you should be able to define you. If it's in God's plans, I want to be part of your life."

ELEVEN

On his morning off, Spencer ran over to the bakery and picked up cinnamon rolls for Hannah and the girls. He also grabbed coffee.

He whistled as he strolled up the walk. Mrs. Greene was sitting on the porch knitting. "You seem very chipper today."

"If I had known you'd be up so early, I would have bought you a coffee."

She tapped the handle of her teacup. "I'm having a spot of tea."

Spencer put down the bag and cup holder and sat across from Mrs. Greene. "How are you today?"

"I didn't sleep well last night. I heard you and Hannah talking in the stairwell."

"I'm sorry."

She waved him off. "No worries. I'm an old lady. We don't sleep well anyway." She tucked in her chin and studied him for a minute. "Oh, don't worry, I wasn't listening. I heard your voices, not the details of your conversation. I had to make sure no one was up to no good."

He smiled.

"You and the Amish girl are getting close." It was more a statement than a question.

"Hannah's not Amish."

"She grew up Amish, she'll always be Amish in her heart."

"Why do you say that?"

"Oh, I've seen plenty of young Amish people get caught up with *Englischers*. That's what they call us. They always go back to their community."

"Always?"

"From what I can see from my corner of the world." She took a long sip of her tea.

Hannah stepped onto the porch with her nieces. Hannah and Spencer locked gazes, and something zinged his heart. Oh, he was in deep. Mrs. Greene cleared her throat. He shifted his gaze to hers. "But what do I know. My corner of the world is pretty small."

He felt himself smile. Then he remembered the cinnamon buns and coffee. He got to his feet. "I brought you breakfast."

Hannah rested her hands on the backs of each girl's head. Emma smiled brightly whereas Sarah seemed shy, but not quite so angry anymore. "How nice of you. We were going into town. It's a beautiful morning."

Mrs. Greene stood and gathered her teacup and

breakfast dish. "Please, all of you, sit and enjoy the porch. I have some chores to do."

"Don't let us chase you away," Hannah said.

Mrs. Greene waved as she was inclined to do. "I'll enjoy relaxing out here once I know my chores are done." Spencer held the screen door open for her.

He pulled out the napkins and put them in front of two spots at the small table tucked in the corner. Hannah took the coffee from him and inhaled deeply. "This is wonderful." He pulled out a roll with a napkin and handed it to her. "Thanks so much."

As they enjoyed their breakfast, a man dressed in a suit walked up the pathway. Everyone stopped eating and watched him. Spencer met him at the bottom of the steps.

Spencer crossed his arms and widened his stance. "Can I help you?"

The man's gaze shifted toward Hannah. "I'm looking for Miss Wittmer."

Hannah stood. "I'm Miss Wittmer."

The man stepped forward, his hand outstretched, then seemed to think better of it. "I'm Frank Jones, a lawyer with Jones and Jones." He tipped his head. "My father," he added, clarifying the second Jones, a question he must have been asked a lot.

"How can we help you, Mr. Jones?" Spencer shifted his stance to block Jones from advancing on Hannah.

"I have been retained by the Lapp family."

Hannah swiped the back of her hand across her forehead. "I don't understand. Why?"

"They plan to gain custody of their nieces." He reached into his pocket and consulted a piece of paper. "A Sarah and Emma Lapp."

Spencer felt a muscle working in his jaw. "Mr. Jones, as you can see, we're enjoying breakfast. Perhaps you can speak to Miss Wittmer—" he tipped his head toward the little girls "—at a more appropriate time."

"When would be a more…ah…appropriate time?"

Spencer dug into his back pocket and opened his wallet. He extracted a business card and handed it to Mr. Jones. "Contact me at this number, and we'll arrange an appointment."

A smug look settled on Mr. Jones's features. "Can't Miss Wittmer speak for herself?"

"You heard the sheriff. You need to go through him to get to me." Hannah stepped down onto the walkway. "And you can tell the Lapps that I will never hand over these girls. I'm surprised they would even employ a lawyer."

Mr. Jones straightened his tie and seemed to stand a little straighter. "I offered to represent them pro bono."

Spencer's eyebrows shot up. "You approached them?"

"Their ignorance of the law makes them ripe targets to be taken advantage of."

"By you?" Spencer couldn't hold back his retort. "No sense wasting an opportunity to get your name in the paper," he mumbled.

Mr. Jones lifted a thin eyebrow, never taking his gaze from Hannah's face. Spencer fisted his hand. "Here's my card." The lawyer reached into the inner pocket of his suit coat and offered her his card. "I'll be filing the paperwork this afternoon. I expect the judge to order you and the children not to leave town."

Hannah felt dizzy and her vision narrowed on the man's cheap suit and bad comb-over as he sauntered down the walkway.

"Can he do that?"

Spencer turned to the girls. "Emma and Sarah, Mrs. Greene has a great tree for climbing over there." He pointed to a low tree with thick branches sprouting from the earth like an octopus's tentacles. "Why don't you check it out?"

Emma bolted down the porch steps. Spencer turned to Sarah. "Would you mind making sure your sister doesn't fall out of the tree?"

Sarah rolled her eyes. "You're sending us away so you can talk in private."

"You're right. We have grown-up things to figure out. Now go watch Emma. Thank you."

Sarah stuck out her lower lip. Her shoulders slumped and she stomped across the porch. Hannah let out a long sigh as she settled down on the wicker couch. "Ah…she'll fit into the English world, yet. And to think she's just a preteen." She shook her head.

Spencer sat across from her. Hannah watched Emma straddle a branch only five feet off the ground. Sarah leaned against the trunk and crossed her arms.

"I know nothing about raising kids in the Amish world, or in this one."

Spencer gave her a look of approval. "You didn't do too badly just now."

"What am I going to do?"

"You knew eventually the courts would have to get involved to decide guardianship for the girls… now that John's body has been found."

"I didn't think the Lapps would use the court system against me. They're going to fight me on this. It's not the Amish way." She placed her palms together and tucked them between her knees. "You were a lawyer once. How likely are they to gain custody?"

"I didn't practice family law. But I can contact someone in Buffalo who can help you." He reached over and patted her knee. "This Jones guy probably read about your brother-in-law's death in the paper and the circumstances surrounding your sister's death and thought he'd make a name for himself."

"I'm going to have to get a job and get the girls

enrolled in school if I hope to stand a chance of gaining permanent custody. Classes start in a few days."

Spencer met her gaze. "Are you sure you want to do this?"

"Raise my sister's daughters?"

"Yes."

"Of course." She couldn't understand why Spencer was asking her this.

"You could give them to the Lapps. I'm sure they'd do well by them."

"My sister wanted me to make sure they were cared for."

"What if making sure they were cared for meant giving them to another family? An Amish family."

Hannah pressed the tips of her fingers to her lips. "I've thought a lot about it. The girls would be better off with me than with the Lapps." She thought back to how stern Fannie Mae had been with the girls. How rigid Lester seemed. Was there anything wrong with being strict? Good parents were strict.

"Sometimes when you do something because you think it's the right thing, you become resentful," he said.

"You know this from experience?"

"Exactly. I had so many people around me, demanding things from me. It was only after I took this job in Apple Creek that I finally felt like I was doing what I was meant to do."

"You are blessed." She closed her eyes briefly, then looked at Spencer. "Growing up Amish, you don't think as a kid about what you're supposed to do in life. You're expected to toe the line. Live life much as your parents did. You generally don't walk around wondering what you should do with your life to make you happy."

Spencer laughed. "Cuts down on a lot of the teenage angst."

Hannah couldn't help but laugh in response. "Not exactly. My father was always hard on me. Harder than he was on Ruthie. My mother recently told me why." She shrugged. "I don't want to betray my *mem*'s confidence, but growing up, feeling like I could do no right, makes me want to do the right thing for my nieces. I need to raise them." She threaded her fingers and squeezed. "I know with certainty that I need to raise these girls. I pray God gives me the wisdom to help them through the transition from farm life to—" she held up her hands "—to this life."

Spencer smiled brightly. "Looks like you have your answer."

Her eyes narrowed. "You baited me. You wanted to force me to realize what I wanted to do."

Smiling, he lifted his hands. "You got me. Now you can stop questioning yourself."

"Yes, it's time I stopped waffling."

"Will you stay in Apple Creek?" She thought she noticed a bit of eager anticipation in his voice.

"I want to be here for *Mem*. I can't leave her." Indecision weighed on her. "As it is, I feel horrible about leaving her alone on the farm." She rubbed her hand along the back of her neck. "My *mem* is a much stronger woman than I ever gave her credit for. She made sacrifices in the hopes of giving me a better life. Besides, I have to stay until Emma and Sarah's guardianship is resolved."

Spencer stood and leaned over, brushing a kiss on her warm forehead.

A little girl's laugh made her look up. Emma was covering her mouth, stifling a giggle. Spencer strolled over and ruffled Emma's hair. "What's so funny, little one?"

Emma spun around, her skirt billowing in a colorful cloud and she raced away from Spencer and joined her sister by the tree.

Later that day, Spencer drove Hannah and her nieces to the Lapp farm to visit Mrs. Wittmer. He had to go to the farm anyway to meet a fire investigator.

"I'll be out back." Spencer tipped his head toward the charred structure that once was the Lapps' barn. Chief Fire Investigator Carl Owen's truck was already parked alongside the barn. Spencer had called his old friend from Buffalo to help him pin down the cause of the fire.

"Okay." A faint smile played on Hannah's lips. "I'll take the girls in to see their granny."

Spencer cupped her elbow. "I can take you guys home whenever you want."

"Thank you." Hannah stretched and brushed a kiss on his cheek. "I don't know what I'd do without you."

Spencer was about to say something witty when Sarah called out impatiently, "Come on, Aunt Hannah." Emma ran ahead to her grandmother's door.

Hannah shrugged, a hint of embarrassment glistened in her eyes. She turned and followed her nieces inside.

Spencer strode across the yard to the barn. He stopped at the edge of the structure, not trusting that it would be sound. The smell of charred wood hung in the air.

"Ah, you made it." Carl came around the corner, a clipboard in his hand.

Spencer extended his hand. "Thanks for driving in from Buffalo. I appreciate it."

"What's all the fuss about a barn fire?" Carl gave him a who's-the-girl smile. "Don't tell me you've fallen for a nice Amish girl?"

Spencer laughed. "Does she look Amish?" He decided to be purposely vague. Most of his friends from Buffalo had razzed him when he told them he was moving to Apple Creek. Amish country.

"Not exactly," Carl had to admit.

Spencer tipped his chin toward the barn. "What did you find?"

"Patterns of an accelerant on the wood. The fire was set intentionally."

Spencer's shoulders tensed. "Not a case of someone tipping over a kerosene lamp?"

"Not unless the person shook the kerosene lamp before dropping it." Carl stepped inside the footprint of the barn and pointed to darker marks on the partial walls. "See, that's where the accelerant raced across the walls. Look around. A barn is ripe for a devastating fire." Carl tucked his pen in his shirt pocket. "Got some leads on this one?"

"Maybe." Samuel had claimed he saw John Lapp at the barn shortly before it went up in flames. However, a dead man wasn't able to give up secrets.

"The owner of the house had been out here asking questions. Before you got here."

Spencer narrowed his gaze.

Carl consulted something on his clipboard. "A guy named Lester Lapp."

"Hmm… He didn't take long to claim ownership."

"Claimed he was moving in and had stopped by to make a few repairs."

Spencer ran a hand along his jaw, considering something. "Want to take a ride with me? Give me fresh eyes on something?"

"Sure. I'll follow you in my truck."

Spencer drove over to the Fisher's home and parked along the road. The two men climbed the porch steps, their boots creaking on the planks. Through the screen door Rebecca could be heard pleading with someone.

He held up his hand to silence Carl who looked like he was about to make a crack about the Amish.

"Neh, neh..." Rebecca pleaded. "You cannot..."

Alarmed that a domestic situation was getting out of control, Spencer knocked loudly on the door. It grew quiet inside.

Too quiet.

"Mrs. Fisher, it's Sheriff Maxwell."

"Go away," she hollered.

"Is everything okay in there?"

A rustling sounded from inside the log home. He could hear hushed whispers from deep in the house. All his senses went on high alert.

"Mrs. Fisher, I need you to come to the door. *Now.*" Spencer pointed to the side of the house. Carl nodded and backed off the porch.

A second later, Rebecca appeared at the door, smoothing her hand along her bonnet. The panic and worry in her eyes had him searching the entryway behind her.

"Who were you talking to?"

Rebecca studied the hardwood floor at her feet.

"Is your husband home?"

The young woman's head snapped up, her eyes wide with fear, definitely fear. "Oh, no. Willard's not home." She glanced around Spencer, and her eyes landed on Carl standing in the front yard. "My husband should be home soon. You're only making things worse. Please leave, he doesn't like to deal with outsiders."

"Why is that?" Spencer searched her face. "I find most Amish to be quite chatty in town. Why is Willard Fisher against fraternizing with his non-Amish neighbors?"

She stepped onto the porch, her eagerness to have them gone radiating off her. "My husband will be home soon."

"Then we'll wait." Spencer could feel his friend Carl watching them.

"I'm going to take a walk around back," Carl said.

Spencer nodded briefly but didn't say anything.

"Sheriff Maxwell. You have only been kind to me and my son, but I need you to leave. Willard—" she shook her head "—Willard won't like that you're here."

"We can protect you if you're afraid of your husband."

Rebecca's lower lip began to quiver. "I don't need protection from my husband." Her tone was not convincing. Behind her in the house, her two younger children watched with wide eyes.

Spencer lowered his voice so as not to scare the children. "Have you heard about a few of the elders having their beards cut off in break-ins?"

Rebecca's eyes widened. "Of course. This is a small town. Such a terrible thing." She made a tsking noise with her mouth.

"Do you know anything about it?"

A deep line marred her forehead. *"Neh. Neh."*

She nudged his forearm directing him toward the steps. Anger with a hint of apology flashed in her eyes. "You must go, *please*."

Spencer descended the steps. Carl appeared at the side of the house holding an angry Samuel by the forearm. "Is this who you were looking for?"

"Yeah." Spencer shot a sideways glance at Rebecca.

"He has done nothing wrong. *Please*."

"I only want to talk to him. Find out what he knows about the fire in the Lapps' barn."

Samuel's eyes grew bright. "I didn't…"

Rebecca ran down the steps, the fabric of her skirt flapping around her legs. "Samuel is a *gut* boy. He told you he saw John Lapp there. He knows nothing else."

"Let the boy talk," Spencer said, watching Samuel carefully. "You and your *mem* were arguing when we arrived. What about?"

"I'm leaving." Samuel pushed the dirt around with the toe of his boot, like he always seemed to do when confronted with authority.

"You can't leave." Rebecca's tone bordered on hysteria.

"I can't stay."

"Why not?" Spencer gestured to Carl to let the boy go.

Samuel yanked his arm away and narrowed his gaze at Carl. "I'm sick of this town."

"Samuel! You cannot leave the Amish faith."

"Why not? *Dat* did."

"He came back. He made a mistake. The world is filled with wicked things. You cannot ignore everything we've taught you."

Feeling the situation escalating, Spencer decided to take it down a notch. "Samuel, if you love your mother, you'll stay put. At least tonight. The morning often brings a brighter outlook."

Samuel twisted his mouth in indecision.

"How about this," Spencer reasoned. "Give it seven days. If you still want to leave, I'll drive you wherever you want to go."

Rebecca gasped.

"Would you rather he ran away on foot tonight? It will be dark soon."

Rebecca lifted a shaky hand to her mouth. "I don't want him to leave. Ever."

"You can't tell *Dat*. I can't stay if you're going to tell *Dat*."

Spencer turned to Rebecca. She bowed her head, but didn't say anything.

"I will keep your secret, Samuel, if you promise not to run away in the middle of the night."

Samuel adjusted his hat low on his forehead to hide his eyes. Something in Spencer's gut told him Samuel Fisher harbored more than one secret.

TWELVE

"Mem, are you sure you're feeling okay? You look a little pale." Hannah's mother's seemingly frail health had her visiting again the next afternoon. Spencer had dropped her off and promised to return in an hour. Hannah plucked at her T-shirt as she sat in the rocker next to her mother near a woodstove pumping out excessive heat on the warm summer afternoon.

"I'm a little chilled, that's all." Her mother ran her hands up and down her thin arms.

"I feel bad leaving you here."

"It's a little quiet. But I understand Fannie Mae and Lester will be moving in soon." A look Hannah couldn't quite decipher swept across her features.

"I registered the girls for school this morning," Hannah said, eager to change the topic.

Her mother stared straight ahead. "At the public school in town?"

"Yes, and their new teachers gave them a few books to read. They're excited. They decided to stay home and read. Our landlady, Mrs. Greene, is keeping them company." Hannah omitted that she wanted to talk to her mother in private.

"I should be the one spending time with my granddaughters." Her mother pressed her fingers to her temple and winced.

"You could return to the wild days of your youth and move into the apartment with me." Hannah tried to lighten the mood.

Her mother raised her hands. "I wasn't baptized then. If I left now, I'd be shunned. As it is, I'm not sure the bishop will like you visiting me so often now that you've taken the girls away."

Anger warmed Hannah's cheeks, reminiscent of the days she'd been fuming over her father's strict discipline. "How many of your neighbors have stopped by since the fire? Since you've been left alone out here? The bishop has to understand I need to look in on you."

Her mother lifted her face, a look of surprise on her pale features. "Several of the neighbors have stopped by." She reached over and picked up her knitting project from the table next to her rocker.

Embarrassment replaced Hannah's anger. "I just assumed…"

"Have you forgotten what a tight-knit community Apple Creek is? My friends have been checking in on me." Her knitting needles clicked as her hands deftly worked the yarn. "They didn't come around as much when you were here, because they knew you were here."

"I should have known."

Her mother tipped her head, observing her as if for the first time since she arrived. "You have a lightness to your hair."

Hannah grabbed her ponytail and inspected it. "Oh, I had highlights put in a while ago. They're mostly washed out."

"Is that expensive?"

Hannah laughed. "Probably more than I should have spent on a bank teller's salary."

Her mother smiled. "There is a big world out there, isn't there?"

"I wouldn't really know. Mine wasn't too big."

"When I met your father, your biological father, I imagined a world outside the farm for the first time. It was an exciting, heady time." A hint of a smile touched her lips. "Your father had a lot of dreams. He was in college studying to be an accountant. I thought it was interesting you had a job at a bank."

"I'm sorry I never met him."

Her mother fidgeted with the string of yarn, but stopped working the needles. "If he hadn't died, our life would have been completely different." Her mother's lips pressed into a thin line. "God works in mysterious ways. You were a blessing. I learned to be content with my life here. Eli spared me a life of shame." She put the knitting aside. "I hope you've had time to forgive Eli for being stern with you. Without him, I would have been lost. *We* would have been lost. I can't imagine my life as a single mom in a world that was mostly foreign to me."

"I do forgive him." The words sprang from Hannah's mouth. Yes, she did forgive him. It was rather freeing. How could she not forgive the man for allowing her sweet mother to return to the life she cherished?

"I hope you can forgive me, too."

"You've done nothing wrong, *Mem*."

"I should have intervened when it came to your father."

"*Mem*, that is not the Amish way. A wife defers to her husband."

Her mother bit her lower lip but didn't say anything.

Realizing her mother felt uncomfortable, Hannah smiled and asked, "Can I do anything for you while I'm here?"

"I ran out of strawberry jam. Can you get a jar out of the basement?"

"Absolutely." Hannah got to her feet.

She walked through the kitchen and opened the basement door. She descended the wood steps, remembering how terrified she was of these steps and the gaps between them when she was a kid. She hadn't even seen the horror movies that she had as an adult to instill such irrational fear.

She crossed the dirt floor of the basement to

get to her mother's stored collection of jams and vegetables. For some inexplicable reason, the tiny hairs on her arms prickled to life. Dark shadows crept out from every corner and underneath the stairs. The two windows were mud caked, blocking natural light.

Hannah sucked in a deep breath and immediately regretted it when the musty scent filled her lungs. She grabbed a jar of jelly and ran up the stairs, taking them two at a time. She slammed the basement door shut, feeling a little silly for letting a few shadows get the best of her.

In the light of day, she looked at the label. Grape. "*Mem*, is grape okay?"

"I prefer strawberry. Am I out of strawberry?"

Hannah pushed back her shoulders. A little voice said, *The least you can do is get your mother some strawberry jam.*

"I'll check. I grabbed the wrong one."

"Take the flashlight from the kitchen drawer."

Hannah rustled through the drawer and found a flashlight. Feeling its heftiness in her hand, she opened the door and descended the stairs. She wasn't sure if the flashlight was a good or a bad thing. It illuminated only what was in its beam, leaving the rest of the basement in darker shadows as her eyes strained to adjust.

She found her mother's storage closet and

pointed the flashlight at the line of jars. She found the strawberry jam.

Something tugged on her hair. Terror clawed at her throat. She couldn't move her head. Someone had her ponytail in his grasp. A scream died in her throat. She fought against his hold and brought up the flashlight to hit him. Metal crashed on bone. A deep groan whispered across her cheek. A ripping sound tore through the confined space. She was suddenly free. She pushed back and spun around. Dark shadows dipped and dodged. She stumbled forward and landed hard on one knee. The flashlight rolled out of her grip and the beam of light swept across a cobwebbed corner.

Her hair was gone.

"Who's there?" A knot formed in her throat. She slowly lifted the beam of her flashlight. Every nerve ending fired to life.

Footsteps pounded up the stairs. A door slammed.

Heart in her throat, Hannah scrambled to her feet and bolted up the stairs.

Her mother.

She turned the door handle, but it didn't budge. Her pulse whooshed in her ears. Hannah slammed her shoulder against the door and was rewarded with splintering pain that radiated through her shoulder and neck.

She pounded on the door, frantic. *"Mem! Mem!"*

Terror narrowed her throat. She closed her eyes

briefly and sent up a silent prayer to protect her mother. Her poor, defenseless mother.

From somewhere in Hannah's mother's house Spencer heard a pounding. Without knocking, he rushed into the house. Mrs. Wittmer was moving things around, looking in drawers, in baskets, and on every flat surface. She was shaking, frail.

"What's going on?" The door at the end of the kitchen vibrated from pounding.

"Hannah's stuck in the basement. I can't imagine what happened to the key or how she got stuck down there."

"Are you okay?" Spencer hollered through the door, flattening his palm against the surface as if he could better connect with her.

"Yes. Yes. Open the door, please." Hannah's tone was desperate, panicked. She stopped pounding.

"Hold on." He jiggled the handle.

Mrs. Wittmer grew more agitated the longer she searched for the key.

"Do you have a screwdriver?"

"Mr. Wittmer has a toolbox—" she looked up slowly "—in the barn."

"It's okay." Spencer placed a reassuring hand on Mrs. Wittmer's shoulder. "I have a toolbox in my truck." He pulled out a chair at the table and encouraged Mrs. Wittmer to sit.

He tapped the door with his palm. "Hannah, I'll be right back. I need to get tools from the truck."

"Hurry, *please.*"

Was she crying? Maybe she was claustrophobic and overreacting to being trapped.

Spencer hustled out the door and returned a few minutes later with his toolbox. When he finally tapped out the bolt from the hinges, he pried the door open and leaned it against the wall. Hannah practically fell up the last stair. She dipped her head, resting her forehead on his broad chest. He gave her back a gentle rub. "Are you…?" The last word died on his lips. He threaded his fingers through her shorn locks. Anger burned his gut. Someone had cut off her ponytail.

He gripped her forearms and placed her at arm's length. "Who did this to you?"

"I don't know." She tugged the elastic out of her hair and it fell in uneven layers. "I slugged him with the flashlight."

He couldn't help but smile. "Good for you."

Spencer inspected the door frame. On the floor he noticed a narrow piece of wood. "He must have stuffed this piece of wood in the door frame to jam the door closed."

"Your hair?" her mother whispered. "Maybe it's the same man who's been attacking the elders. Cutting their beards."

John Lapp had been their primary focus in those cases.

But John was dead.

Maybe John hadn't been responsible for terrorizing Hannah.

Or maybe John hadn't worked alone.

"I didn't see his face." Hannah let out a long breath between tight lips. "I need air." She pushed past Spencer and ran out the back door onto the porch. Spencer followed. She braced her arms on the railing and peered into the yard. "Where did he go?" she asked in a faraway voice. "Where did he go?"

"How do you know he went outside? I need to check the house."

"Go, check the house, but I heard the back door slam. My guess is he's long gone."

After checking the entire house and the house next door, Spencer returned and gave them the all clear. Hannah's mother had joined her on the porch.

"*Mem*, you can't stay here."

Hannah's mother shook her head. "This is my home."

Hannah held up a shorn lock. "Look what he did to me."

"God will protect me. I cannot live in your world."

Spencer felt like he was intruding on their conversation. He touched Hannah's shoulder. "Your mother is probably right. If the person you encountered in the basement wanted to hurt your mother, he could have done it at any time. *You* are the person he's targeting."

THIRTEEN

Emma raced up the stairs to the second-floor apartment ahead of Hannah. Emma bounced on the balls of her feet with impatience at the door, waiting for her aunt to unlock it.

"You had a good first day of school, huh?"

"It was awesome," Emma said, shifting from foot to foot. "They have a library, and I can take books home anytime I want. I have to remember to bring them back. I can't keep them forever."

Hannah slipped the key into the lock and heard the dead bolt click. "You know they have bathrooms at school?" She smiled at her niece.

"I was so excited to get on the bus to come home, I forgot." Emma shot past Hannah and disappeared into the apartment.

Hannah paused at the door, waiting for Sarah to climb the steps. Her older niece was harder to read. "How was your day?"

She shrugged.

"So, it wasn't so bad?"

"A girl told me I looked plain."

Hannah angled her head to study her niece. She reached out and dragged a strand of her niece's long hair through her fingers. "You are a beautiful girl."

Sarah scrunched her nose. Either her niece didn't believe her aunt, or she had been offended. The Amish were a humble people. Just because Hannah had moved Sarah out of Amish country didn't mean Sarah relinquished her modest sensibilities.

Sarah followed Hannah to the kitchen and tossed her backpack down on one of the stools.

"Do you think you could grow to like living here?" Hannah desperately wanted her niece to say, "Yes." Instead, all she got was another shrug.

Emma raced into the kitchen and hopped up on a stool.

"Did you wash your hands?"

Emma rolled her eyes. "Of course. I love the strawberry soap." She took a deep whiff of her hands. "Can I have a snack now?"

Hannah was grateful at least one of her nieces had adjusted readily. She grabbed a bag of baby carrots from the fridge and filled a small bowl. Emma happily chomped on a carrot, and Sarah picked one up and inspected it. Hannah leaned her elbows on the counter. "I love you guys."

Emma slipped off the stool and ran over to Hannah, wrapping an arm around her waist. "Love you, too, Aunt Hannah. And I really like your haircut." Hannah had had to go into town and get her hair cut and styled after the ponytail incident in her mother's basement.

"Thank you." She dragged her fingers through her hair, still unaccustomed to the short bob, but it felt freeing.

"Can I get one?" Emma smoothed her long ponytail over her shoulder and inspected the ends with crossed eyes.

Hannah laughed. "Sure, if you'd like." Her gaze drifted to Sarah. "Maybe we can take a few inches from your hair, too, Sarah."

Alarm flitted across Sarah's bright blue eyes.

"We don't have to," Hannah reassured her.

Sarah pressed her lips together, and her nose twitched. She sniffed. "I miss *Mem*."

"I miss her terribly, too. She was my little sister."

"Like me. I'm the little sister," Emma said, jubilantly.

"And your big sister will keep an eye on you."

"Yeah, if it wasn't for me—" Sarah sniffed a few times "—Emma would have left her backpack on the playground when it came time to board the bus."

"I left it by the school door. I wouldn't have left it behind," Emma said in a petulant tone.

"That's not where I found it. It was behind the tree near the front walk. You're not supposed to leave the playground."

"I didn't." Emma flared her nose and shook her head at her big sister.

"Stop arguing. Emma, you have to make sure you don't lose your things." Hannah couldn't afford to replace backpacks. She had a job interview with the credit union in town tomorrow. Hopefully her finances would turn around then. The few thousand dollars from the sale of her car wouldn't hold out forever.

Hannah scooped up the floral backpack Emma had picked out. She gravitated toward an explosion of colors now that she wasn't restricted to her plain clothing. Sarah's navy backpack sat next to her little sister's. Obviously, Sarah was going to take more time.

Hannah planted the bag on the stool and unzipped it. She pulled out Emma's take-home folder with its glossy cover of cute kittens, a staple of the elementary school set. She opened the folder, and her heart stuttered. An envelope with Hannah's name scratched in bold letters poked out from one of the pockets.

Relax. Perhaps the teacher had sent home a note.

Her pulse thumped in her ears. The jagged writing didn't resemble the neat, cursive handwriting of the teacher who had given Hannah a school-supply list last week.

Mouth growing dry, Hannah turned her back to the girls and slipped her finger under the flap of the envelope. Brown hair poked out of it. Nausea clawed at her throat. Emma was talking, but her voice sounded as if it were coming through a tunnel.

"One minute," Hannah said absentmindedly as she moved toward the window for better lighting. She pulled out a square piece of yellow paper with the words, "Go Home, *Englischer*."

Hannah stuffed the paper back into the envelope with the hair—*her hair*. She cleared her throat and tried to keep her tone calm. "Sarah, help your sister get another snack. There's milk in the fridge and cookies in the pantry. I have to make a phone call." The walls of the small apartment grew closer, and a sheen of sweat slicked her palms as she fumbled for her cell phone in her purse.

Hannah was only vaguely aware of Sarah's complaining. Hannah stepped into the stairwell and dialed Spencer's cell phone. She knew he wasn't home.

He answered on one ring.

"The person who attacked me on the farm is at it again." She fingered the soft strands of hair. "He is not going to stop until I'm gone."

Happy to be home, Spencer strolled up the walkway and found Hannah standing behind the screen door.

"Hey."

"Hey."

"This creep is never going to stop, is he? I thought our problems were over when John died." Hannah's voice trembled. "Maybe I'm doing the wrong thing. Maybe I should let Lester and Fannie Mae raise the girls. Maybe then all this would stop. The girls would be safe."

Spencer climbed the porch steps, watching Hannah carefully. Fear radiated from her eyes. He opened the screen door and cupped Hannah's elbow. "You are not going to let this person chase you away."

For selfish reasons, he didn't want her to leave. But was the choice his?

With a shaky hand she offered him an envelope. He opened it and read the note and cursed under his breath. "Let me lock this in my truck."

When he returned to the porch, Hannah was sitting on the top step, slumped against the post. Her new short bob hung forward, hiding her face. He brushed his fingers across her knee and sat next to her.

Hannah looked up. Her eyes glistened in the late-afternoon sun. "I'm afraid."

A memory slammed into him. Another mom. Another time. Another family in jeopardy.

"I'm going to make sure nothing happens to you and the girls."

Spencer had made that promise before. He had promised fourteen-year-old Daniel's mother he would make sure the boy was safe. And he mistakenly thought that keeping him out of gangs would protect him. He hadn't counted on finding Daniel dead on the sidewalk outside the corner store. The milk he had purchased for his little brother slung in a plastic bag, its handles twisted around his wrist. All because he had worn the wrong color that day.

Some things were out of his control.

"How are you going to do that? You can't be with me and the girls all the time," she said, as if she were reading his mind.

No, no, he couldn't. Spencer wanted to stand and punch the post, but instead he drew in a deep breath through his nose.

Think rationally.

"Whoever is doing this wants you to leave Apple Creek. Who has a motive?"

Hannah flicked the ends of her hair. "Someone who is willing to lurk in my mother's basement and cut off my ponytail isn't exactly dealing with a full deck." She tucked her hands under her thighs and shuddered.

"Who would want you to leave?" Spencer repeated.

Hannah slowly lifted her eyes. "Fannie Mae and Lester Lapp?"

"You've all but given them the farm and the land they wanted," Spencer said, thinking out loud.

"They want the girls." All the blood rushed out of her face, leaving her deathly white. "But doesn't this seem too radical? It made more sense—if you can call it that—when we thought John was harassing me. Could both brothers be equally ruthless?"

Spencer rubbed the back of his neck. "I'll talk to Lester again."

Sitting on the porch step, Hannah leaned forward and covered her face with her hands. "I don't know how much more of this I can take." Her shoulders shook, then she stilled. She pulled her hands away and stared at him. "The person who chopped my hair is probably one of the men who cut the elders' beards. I can't see Lester being part of that group."

"Do we ever truly know what's in someone's heart?"

"What have you uncovered about this radical group?" Hannah stretched her legs in front of her and crossed her ankles.

"They left notes in the Amish homes where they cut the beards." Spencer shifted toward her, icy dread flowing through her veins.

Hannah drew her legs in and hugged her knees. "Notes?"

"The notes were cryptic. One in particular read, 'remove a wicked person from our midst.'" Spencer scratched his arm. "The Amish men who were attacked didn't want to talk, and other Amish men claimed the note might refer to the Amish custom of staying separate or apart from outsiders." He shrugged. "John Lapp had been one of our suspects, but he's dead."

Hannah let out a heavy sigh. "I called the school. No one saw anyone hanging around the playground at dismissal." She scratched the top of her head. "Perhaps whoever did this blended in."

"I'll look into it further." Careful to keep his

expression void of emotion, Spencer said, "I have friends and family in Buffalo you and the girls can stay with until we catch this guy."

Spencer followed Hannah's gaze as she scanned the neighborhood. Across the street, an older gentleman took his garbage out and dumped it in a trash can at the side of his house. A few doors down a thin, wiry man cut the grass with a plug-in lawn mower.

Hannah met his gaze. "My harasser could be anyone, couldn't it?"

Spencer shook his head. "Not anyone. We have to look for someone who has a reason to want you to leave."

Hannah bit her lower lip. "What if it's Samuel, angry at me for getting him in trouble with his father?"

Spencer had considered Samuel, but ranked him low on the suspect list. "The tire-slashing incident occurred before you caught Samuel reading in the barn."

"What if my brother-in-law started to harass me and Samuel continued it?"

"He doesn't strike me as that kind of kid. But we should consider all possibilities."

"I like Samuel." She laughed, a mirthless sound. "I might be too naive, but I hate to think a nice young Amish boy would be set on revenge. That's not something I've seen a lot in the Amish community. They foster forgiveness."

"The Amish are human. They aren't perfect."

She threaded her fingers through her hair. "Tell me about it."

"What about his father, Willard Fisher?"

"He's strict, but again, that's not unusual in an Amish home." She lifted her eyes heavenward.

"I'll reach out to Rebecca, again." Spencer ran a few scenarios through his head.

"No, you can't put her in jeopardy. If Willard gets wind of this…"

Hannah's phone rang. Her brow creased. She reached into her pocket and pulled it out. "Hello." Her expression grew startled. "Yes. Okay. I'll be right there."

She ended the call and jumped to her feet.

"What's wrong?"

"*Mem*. She's in the hospital."

The hospital doors whirred open. "Are you sure Mrs. Greene doesn't mind keeping the girls again?" Hannah asked as they strode toward the hospital information desk. Her nerves were fried, and she was grateful Spencer was at her side when she had received the phone call from the hospital.

"Mrs. Greene loves the company. Don't worry, I told her to stay inside behind locked doors. I'll have a patrol drive by every thirty minutes." Spencer slowed, and Hannah glanced over at him; the compassion in his eyes touched her heart. "The girls will be safe. No one knows they are in Mrs. Greene's apartment."

A shudder skittered through her. *Please Lord, let them be safe.*

Spencer asked for her mother's hospital room information, and the volunteer at the information desk handed them two purple visitor passes, which they slapped on their T-shirts.

Hannah led the way into her mother's room. She came up short when she found Rebecca sitting in the corner of the room. Her bonnet and gown seemed in stark contrast to the modern room with the TV on the wall and the monitor mounted on a mobile stand next to her mother's bed.

Hannah's gaze shifted to her mother. Her eyes were closed, and her head hung at an awkward angle on the raised head of the hospital bed.

"Is she…?"

"She's sleeping. I don't know any more. The doctor was waiting for family to arrive."

"Did you find her?"

Rebecca nodded. "I brought her an apple pie. When no one answered, I went in. She was unconscious on the kitchen floor."

"She should have never been alone. I should have been there." Panic made her nauseous.

What was she going to do?

"I ran across to the English neighbors. They called an ambulance. I didn't know what else to do." A mix of fear and relief played across Rebecca's face. Hannah's poor, sweet friend.

Hannah touched her friend's arm. *"Denki."*

"You're welcome." Rebecca drew in a deep breath and let it out. "I should get home. Willard will be looking for his dinner. *Mem*'s minding the little ones." Rebecca gave Hannah a watery smile. "Please give your *mem* my best."

Rebecca stiffened when she hugged her. "Thank you again." Hannah gestured to Spencer. "Spencer could drive you home."

"I'd be happy to," Spencer said.

Rebecca shook her head. "I'll call a cab." She walked toward the door, her footsteps quiet on the tile floor. She slowed in the doorway and turned around. "I miss you. I wish you'd come home."

"I can't." The words got lodged in Hannah's throat. "Please forgive me, Rebecca, but I have to lead my own life. I'll make sure Sarah and Emma are raised in faith."

Rebecca's features grew pinched. "You have your *mem* to consider now."

The walls began to sway, and the room seemed suddenly very hot. "I have a lot to figure out." Hannah watched as Rebecca left the room.

Hannah pulled up a chair next to the bed and grabbed her mother's cold hand. She rubbed her thumb across the back of it. Forgetting Spencer was there, she closed her eyes and said a silent prayer. *Thank you for sending Rebecca to look in on*

Mem. Please make her well. She opened her eyes and found Spencer watching her. Fidgeting with the folds of the blankets, she lowered her gaze. *Please help me do what's best for my family. My entire family.*

The sound of the door opening drew her attention. A woman in a white lab coat with a stethoscope draped around her neck walked into the room. If Hannah hadn't been studying the woman's face, she might have missed the fleeting look of confusion.

Hannah pushed to her feet and extended her hand. "I'm Hannah Wittmer. This is my mother." Hannah gently squeezed her mother's hand, trying to explain the familial relationship.

"I'm Dr. Jennings." The slow cadence of her voice left a question floating in the air-conditioned room.

"I'm not Amish. My mother is."

The physician seemed to mentally shake herself. "Your mother's fortunate."

"Oh?"

"She had a grand-mal seizure. Well…she could have suffered more serious consequences if she had been driving a car or…" The doctor's voice trailed off. "I'm sorry. I realize the Amish don't drive cars. It's a good thing she wasn't alone."

Insert knife. Twist.

Hannah let out a shaky breath, not sure what to say.

"We're going to have to run more tests."

Hannah nodded. The tips of her fingers felt numb.

"When are you going to run the tests?" Spencer stepped forward.

"Tomorrow morning. I've scheduled a CT scan."

Hannah felt Spencer's firm hand on the small of her back as if to say, "I'm here. I'm not going to leave you."

Her mother squeezed her hand. Hannah leaned in. Her mother was awake. "How do you feel, *Mem*?"

"Gut." She struggled with the blankets and the IV in the back of her hand.

"Leave it be. You're in the hospital. Do you remember anything that happened?"

"One side of my mouth was droopy this morning." Her mother's words were garbled a bit, as if she were struggling to enunciate.

Hannah glanced at the physician, looking for reassurance. But her serious gaze made Hannah's heart stop. She didn't want to say any more for fear of scaring her mother.

"Mrs. Wittmer, I'm your physician. You had a seizure, and we'd like to do more tests in the morning to see what caused it."

Her mother swiped at the wires running into the back of her hand. *"Neh,* I want to go home."

Hannah placed a reassuring hand on her mother's arm. "Please, *Mem*." She searched her mother's eyes.

"Consider it an adventure." She gave her mother a knowing smile.

Her mother gave her a tepid smile in return. "Some adventure." She relaxed into the pillow and closed her eyes.

"I've scheduled the CT scan for 8:00 a.m.," the physician said. "We'll know more then."

A knot tightened in Hannah's gut. Tomorrow they would know more.

Tomorrow.

Hannah couldn't shake the dread buzzing her nerve endings. She reached up and covered Spencer's hand on her shoulder. Without Spencer, she would have surely folded under the pressure.

FOURTEEN

The next morning, Emma held Spencer's hand. She was such an easygoing little kid. Meanwhile, Sarah lagged behind as they meandered the halls of the hospital from the cafeteria to the main lobby. Hannah sat in the corner, her head bowed and her cell phone pressed to her ear. Apparently sensing them, she glanced up and pulled the phone away from her ear. "Hey, there."

"You missed it." Spencer smiled, trying to lighten the mood. "They have the best French toast ever."

"Hmm…" Hannah said, a million miles away. He had seen that look before, the look of a woman trying to make a huge decision. He had seen it in Vicki's eyes before she told him she hadn't signed up to be the girlfriend of a cop.

Spencer shook away the thought. Now was not the time to be selfish. Mrs. Wittmer was currently having a CT scan, and Hannah was nervously awaiting the results. One of the nurses promised she'd come find them in the lobby after Hannah's mother returned from her scan.

Spencer plopped down in the chair next to Hannah and covered her hand with his. "No matter what happens, I'll help you through this."

Hannah slowly shifted in her seat. Her knee brushed his. She scooted back; a weary smile crossed her lips. "Thanks for taking the girls to breakfast."

"My pleasure."

Hannah opened the bag next to her and pulled out a Laura Ingalls Wilder book. She stretched across and handed it to Sarah. "I think you'd enjoy this book. I picked it up in the hospital gift shop."

"*Dat* doesn't like us to read things without his approval." Sarah froze, and her eyes locked on her aunt's as if she had just realized what she said.

"Your mother and I loved this book when we were kids. Since you're missing school today, I think you should at least read." In light of the threatening note found in Emma's backpack, Spencer wanted to keep the girls close.

Sarah took the book and turned it over. She pushed back in her seat and opened the cover. The hope on Hannah's face pierced Spencer's heart. He had never met a stronger woman in his life.

He quietly said a prayer to give her continued strength to deal with whatever was about to unfold with her mother. The idea of praying caught him off guard.

Emma ran over to Hannah. "Do you have a book for me?"

"Of course." From her tote, Hannah produced an early reader with Cinderella on the front. Emma skipped over and plopped down next to her sister.

"Cinderella?" Spencer asked, a smirk tilting his lips.

"Too English?" She laughed. He loved the sound. "I didn't experience the world of Disney princesses until after I left Apple Creek. My favorite was Cinderella." She twisted her thin lips, and something flickered briefly in her eyes. "But we all know fairy tales are just stories."

Spencer leaned in close and couldn't resist kissing her soft cheek. Her shampoo smelled of strawberries. "Maybe I have your glass slipper."

Hannah pulled back, a sad smile on her face. "There are plenty of women who would be a better fit for the slipper. For you."

Something twisted in his gut. He could feel her pulling away. Erecting a wall between them.

"Excuse me, Miss Wittmer." A woman dressed in pale blue scrubs entered the waiting room.

Hannah's eyes radiated fear.

The young nurse clasped her hands and lifted them to her chest. "Your mother is done with her CT scan."

Hannah slowly stood, clutching her hands in front of her much like the nurse had done. "Is my mother okay?"

The nurse lowered her gaze, as if the diamond pattern on the worn blue carpet had suddenly become very fascinating. Spencer's heart broke for Hannah.

"Dr. Jennings would like to talk with you in your mother's hospital room."

Hannah turned slowly, her hand extended to her nieces. "The girls."

"I'm sorry," the nurse said. "No one under sixteen is allowed on the patient floors."

Spencer touched her back. "I'll stay with the girls." He hated that he couldn't go upstairs with her.

Hannah nodded slowly. She kissed Sarah and Emma on top of their heads, the action so deliberate, he sensed she was savoring each moment, as if she knew her world was about to be turned upside down.

Hannah was quiet on the drive to the apartment. It had taken all of her energy to collect the girls from the lobby and make it home without crumbling. Even now that she was home, she was struggling to stay composed.

Thankfully, Spencer read the situation and didn't ask her any questions. Before he disappeared into his apartment across the hall, she had asked him to come back after she had put the girls to bed. She needed to talk to someone, to figure things out, or she feared she'd explode.

As she made mac and cheese for the girls, she forced herself to focus on the moment. Boil water, pour in noodles, stir.

Don't think about Mem.

"Is dinner almost ready? I'm hungry." Emma climbed up on the stool and rested her elbows on the counter.

Hannah reached across and squeezed her small hand. "Almost."

Across the small apartment, Sarah was curled up in the corner chair with her nose in her *Little House on the Prairie* book. Maybe Sarah was more like Hannah than she had thought.

A knock on the door brought Sarah's head up. Hannah smiled. "Let me get that." She crossed the room and rose onto her tiptoes and looked through the peephole.

Spencer.

Hannah unlocked the door and opened it. "Hey, there." His friendly smile was like a warm embrace. He was light to her darkness.

"You're early."

"Looks like I'm just in time."

Hannah glanced over her shoulder at the steam rising over the small pot on the stove. "It's only mac and cheese."

"Sounds good."

Hannah laughed. "Whatever floats your boat. I'll put out another plate."

The four of them enjoyed a quiet dinner. Afterward, the girls retired to their rooms to read. When Hannah came back out, Spencer had already cleared the dinner dishes.

"You're a keeper." As soon as the words came out of her mouth she wished she could call them back. She blinked a few times and took a step back.

He tipped his head but didn't say anything. He had an unnerving way of studying her. He led her to the couch and pulled her down next to him. "Tell me about your mom."

Immediately, tears burned the backs of her eyes, and a thick knot lodged in her throat. She let out a long, slow breath. Spencer ran his thumb across the back of her hand.

She pressed her lips together as if that would stop the tears. One escaped and trailed down her cheek. Spencer cupped her cheek and wiped the tear with his thumb. She leaned into his palm, reveling in its warmth. Comfort.

She reached up and wrapped her fingers around his wrist. "You really are a good guy."

"What's on your mind?" His voice was low and husky.

She bowed her head and studied her lap. She couldn't keep it together and look him in the eyes. "The CT scan revealed—" she cleared her throat "—my *mem* has a brain tumor."

Spencer brushed a kiss across her forehead and pulled her head against his chest. "I'm sorry."

She drew in a deep breath. He smelled clean, a

mixture of soap and a subtle aftershave. She tried to clear her mind, her panic.

After taking a minute to pull herself together, she straightened her back. "They're going to release *Mem* tomorrow. She refuses additional treatment."

Spencer's brow furrowed. "What did the physician say?"

"Dr. Jennings said she wanted to refer my mother to a specialist. She figured they'd want to operate and then follow it up with radiation and chemotherapy. She couldn't say for sure until the specialist reviewed my *mem*'s case."

"Your mother refused?"

"She wants to go home and live in peace."

"What about the seizures?"

"The doctor said she could manage the seizures and pain with medication." Hannah traced a seam in the couch cushion and when she looked up, she met a look of sympathy in Spencer's eyes that was nearly her undoing. "I can't force her to have surgery and undergo radiation. I can't."

"Maybe she'll change her mind."

"I don't think she will."

Spencer rubbed her forearm. "What does this mean?"

"I have to go back. For my mother."

"You're going back? What do you mean?" Spencer was unable to hide the disappointment from his tone.

Hannah tipped her head, purposely avoiding his eyes. "I have to take care of my mother."

"Bring your mother here." His plea was more out of selfishness than practicality.

"I need to do everything I can to make her feel comfortable. If she came here, I'm afraid she'd be shunned." She shrugged and tucked a strand of hair behind her ear. "She's a good Amish woman. I don't want to cause her any more undue stress at this time."

"How...?" He wanted to ask her how she planned to return to the Amish community after her grand exit, but he could see from the look on her face that she had no idea. Yet she was determined to do it.

After sitting for a few minutes with her head in her hands, she stood and paced. "I can't force Lester and Fannie Mae to leave the house." She rubbed her forehead unable to smooth the worry lines. "Maybe..." She fidgeted with the ends of her new short, *English* haircut. It was hard to imagine her as the Amish woman he had greeted on the porch of her childhood home not that long ago. So different than the woman standing in front of him.

He stood and pulled her hand in his. "How can I help?"

"You don't think I'm crazy?" The pain in her eyes pierced his heart.

He dragged his knuckles across her cheek. "You wouldn't be the woman I've come to know, if you didn't take care of your mother when she needed you."

Hannah fell into his embrace and stayed there, longer than he expected. He memorized every detail of the fleeting moment.

Hannah pulled back and looked him in the eye. "What about the girls? I can't confuse them like this. One minute they're Amish, then English, then Amish again." She held him tighter. The frustration rolled off her in waves.

He wanted to ask, *What about me? What about us?* That wasn't important now.

"I'll have to make sure you're secure on the farm." The horrible memory of burning wood filled his nose. "Do you think my moving in with you and your mom would be frowned upon?" Humor tilted his lips.

Hannah patted his arm. "I'm sorry, Spencer. I haven't been fair to you. You're a really good guy."

"I feel a but coming on." He let out a long breath.

Hannah sat on the arm of the couch. "My mother gave up her dreams for me." The intensity in her expression told Spencer there was more to that comment than she was letting on.

Spencer sat on the corner of the coffee table and waited for her to continue her story.

"I don't want to betray my mother's confidence, but I know I can trust you." Hannah relayed the story of how her mother had run away with her English boyfriend and returned to the Amish community after she found herself pregnant and alone. "My *mem* was afraid, but she firmly believed she was doing the best thing for me. She had no way of knowing what waited for her in the outside world once my father died, so she retreated to the familiarity of the Amish. She did that for me."

"But your Amish father didn't treat you well."

"My mother had no way of knowing that would be the case. Her decisions were made with my best interests at heart." Hannah slid off the arm of the couch and slouched into the deep cushions. "I owe my mother this much. I need to let her live the last days of her life in her home."

"I'll go back."

Spencer pivoted around the corner of the coffee table. Sarah stood in her pink pj's looking very much like any other nine-year-old girl. The only thing that hinted at her Amish-ness was her hair, tightly pleated in a braid down her back.

Hannah scooted to the edge of the cushion, but didn't stand, perhaps afraid of spooking Sarah. "I thought you were starting to like school."

Sarah's lips twitched. "I want to be with Granny."

"Did you hear us talking…about Grandma?"

Sarah's face crumbled. She rushed over to Hannah and fell into her arms. Hannah closed her eyes, and a tear slipped down her cheek. Spencer looked away.

"Do you think Emma will be okay with going back?"

Sarah nodded without lifting her head. "She's little. She'll be okay as long as she's with you."

"Thank you, sweetie." Hannah patted Sarah's back. "Thank you." On the second thank-you she met and locked eyes with Spencer. He knew how much Sarah's words of support meant to Hannah. And just how much he'd miss living across the hall from this little family.

FIFTEEN

Hannah grabbed her mother's elbow, bony under her touch. It seemed she had lost a few pounds since going into the hospital three days ago. Dr. Jennings had worked wonders in allowing her mother to stay in the hospital long enough to work out her prescription doses. Hannah glanced over her shoulder while Sarah and Emma scooted out of Spencer's truck dressed in their bright-colored skirts and graphic T-shirts.

Butterflies flitted in her stomach. It was a surreal feeling, almost like she was sneaking back into her childhood home, much as she had sneaked out all those years ago.

"Girls, I'm going to get Granny settled, then we'll change our clothes. The bishop is going to stop by." Hannah glanced toward the main house, wondering if Fannie Mae or Lester had moved in yet. An empty space of charred earth marked the spot where the barn had stood. She had heard rumors in town that they were going to have a barn raising in a few weeks, well before the bad weather rolled in.

"Watch the step, *Mem*." Hannah tightened her grip on her mother's arm, stretching out to open the door. A staleness from being closed up for a few days rolled out and greeted them.

Spencer and the girls followed them into the home. She wondered how they'd all live in the small space. Urgency made her mind race. The bishop was supposed to be here before sundown, and she didn't want to cause her mother any more stress. Her Amish clothes were stored away in a chest in the main house. Her mother's discharge had taken longer than expected, and it was late.

Hannah guided her mother to a rocking chair. "How do you feel, *Mem*?"

Her mother's stiff carriage relaxed. "I'm home."

"Maybe you should lie down."

Her mother made a face. "I'm not going to crawl into bed and wait to die."

A crushing weight pressed on Hannah's chest. The walls closed in on her. She opened a window and breathed in the fresh country air. She grabbed a pink bandanna out of her back pocket and wrapped it around her head, holding her hair off her face. Could she do this? Could she return to her Amish roots, for her mother this time?

A knocking sounded on the door. Hannah's heartbeat thudded in her ears. Reflexively she tugged at the hem of her T-shirt. She hadn't had time to change yet.

She watched in slow motion as Spencer opened the door. Lester and Fannie Mae Lapp entered the small space, followed by the bishop. Fannie Mae had an almost hopeful expression on her face.

"You're here already," Hannah said, unable to hide her annoyance.

"We said we'd stop by," Lester said, his steely gaze firmly locked on Hannah. "Fannie Mae and I are living next door now, and my father came by to wish your mother well."

"*Gut* to see you're home, Mrs. Wittmer." The bishop ignored the terse exchange and limped into the small space, leaning heavily on his cane. "How are you feeling?"

"No more fuss. I'm fine." Her mother reached over to grab her knitting, but left it sitting on the table as if even that took too much effort.

Emma and Sarah hung back in the doorway between the sitting room and kitchen. Perhaps they were hiding their English wardrobe from the bishop. Perhaps Hannah should have changed the girls into their dresses before they left the apartment.

Perhaps she'd been trying to delay the inevitable.

Fannie Mae silently gestured to her husband with her eyes. Lester tipped his head toward Hannah. "You've decided to stay?"

Hannah nodded curtly. "We just arrived. We haven't had time to change our clothing."

"Returning to the Amish community means more than wearing plain clothing." The bishop stared at her, his expression hard to read.

"Can we talk outside?" Hannah asked.

The group filed outside. The girls stayed inside to keep their grandmother company.

Hannah was keenly aware of Spencer's presence. She wondered how long he could hang around before he drew the ire of the Amish community.

Hannah took a deep breath and sent up a quick prayer, seeking guidance. "I'll be honest. I *am* struggling with my decision."

"It's not fair to drag my brother's daughters back and forth. They need stability." A muscle ticked in Lester's jaw.

"I'm stuck in a very difficult situation." She swallowed hard as a tingling bit at her fingertips. "My mother is very ill." The words, *She's dying* froze on her lips.

"I need to be here for her."

A very calm expression came over the bishop's face. "*Gott* works in amazing ways. This is what needed to happen to bring you home."

"I pray I'm doing the best thing for my sister's daughters." Hannah shot a sideways look at Lester. Had God truly intended her mother's illness to be the inciting event to force her back to the ways of the Amish for good? Her heart was conflicted.

God had a plan, but could she claim to know it? She had to trust Him.

"The *dawdy haus* is small. The girls can sleep in their old bedroom." Fannie Mae spoke for the first time.

"That's a great idea," Lester agreed.

A nervous knot twisted in Hannah's stomach. The girls were slipping out of her grasp.

"That might be best," the bishop added. "And you'll stay close to your *mem*."

Hannah felt like she had no choice. She'd have to make some concessions if they'd allow her to live among the Amish and care for her mother.

The bishop turned to leave. "Hannah, slow down and be in the moment. I think *Gott* brought you back here for a reason." He took a few more steps and turned back around. "We'll see you at service next week."

Hannah nodded, relieved to have that confrontation behind her. The bishop climbed into the wagon and flicked the reins. The horse took off at an easy trot.

Aware of Lester and Fannie Mae's gazes, Hannah pushed open the door to her mother's home. "Emma, Sarah, come here, please."

The girls appeared in the doorway. Emma smiled and greeted her aunt and uncle. Sarah, as always, was more reserved. Hannah placed her hands on the girls' backs. "How would you two like to sleep in your old bed?"

"I don't want to go to bed yet," Emma complained.

Hannah tapped her back. "Not yet. Later."

Sarah looked up, worry in her eyes, a look that threw Hannah off balance. "Where will you sleep?"

Hannah raised her palm to the room where her mother sat. "Here with Granny. I'll be right here," she added for reassurance.

Fannie Mae held out her arms and each girl took a hand. "Come now. Let's get some proper clothes on and fix your hair." She tugged at one of Emma's curls, a playful tug.

Hannah watched the girls walk away, and her heart broke into a million pieces.

Lester followed his wife, leaving only Spencer and Hannah to watch the last bit of sun dip below the horizon. "Are you okay?" Spencer asked, his voice smooth and comforting.

"I'm grateful I'm here for my mom. Please thank Mrs. Greene again for being so understanding that we broke our lease."

"Don't worry. Focus on your mother."

Hannah nodded, exhaustion making her eyelids scratchy.

"Go. Rest. I'll make sure I have patrols check the property every hour."

"Isn't that overkill?" A chill skittered up her spine. Who was she kidding? All indications were that someone was still after her.

Hannah and Spencer stood looking at one another. The setting sun cast his handsome face in a beautiful glow. Something she didn't dare explore squeezed her heart. Shaking her head to break the spell, she stepped back and looked down and waved her hand up and down her jean-and-T-shirt-clad body. "I'd better change into Amish Hannah."

He smiled. A sad smile. "Hey, Hannah."

She turned back around slowly. "Yeah."

"I don't know if you can trust Lester. Please be careful."

Hannah's eyes grew wide. "Do you think the girls are in danger?"

Spencer shook his head. "You seem to be the primary target."

Target.

She hated the harsh sound of that word. She let out a long sigh. "I have to be here for my mother."

"I know." He sounded resigned.

"For my mother's benefit and out of respect for the Amish community, I have to put my heart into this."

"Your mother needs you." What he didn't say lingered between them.

"Yes, she does." It was time for her to be selfless for her mother, like her mother had been for her.

"I'll make sure you're safe." Something in his eyes told her he needed to keep her safe for reasons all his own.

Spencer climbed the steps of Mrs. Greene's porch, tired, hungry and ready to flop on his couch and forget about the past few days. He had asked the two officers on duty tonight to alternate checking on Hannah at the Lapp farm every hour. He had also convinced Hannah to keep her cell phone close by.

She promised she'd secure the locks at night.

He opened the door and stepped inside the foyer. It smelled like garlic. *At least some things go on as normal.* Mrs. Greene had dinner on the stove.

He smiled when he heard her shuffling footsteps, then the rattling of the doorknob. He suspected she watched all the comings and goings from the recliner positioned near the large window overlooking the yard.

The door opened slowly, and Mrs. Greene peered up at him, her eyes wise from years of experience. "I half expected her to be with you. Didn't think she'd really do it." There was no need to clarify who *she* was.

"Her mother's sick." His heart was heavy, far heavier than it should have been for a woman he had met on the job. Who was he kidding? It had become far more than just a job.

"She's a good daughter, then." Mrs. Greene let her comment hang out there. She was good at eliciting conversation from him even when he didn't feel like talking.

"She's doing what she feels is right."

"And you?" Despite her five-foot stature, she leveled a gaze at him that commanded his attention.

"I liked it better when she was here so I could keep an eye on her."

Mrs. Greene lifted a suspicious eyebrow. "Is that the only reason?"

"I'm afraid you've gotten to know me well, Mrs. Greene." He mirrored her raised eyebrows.

"I raised three sons."

Spencer let out a long breath. "I don't begrudge Hannah for being there for her mother." Even if it meant they couldn't be together.

And his conscience couldn't have him hoping her mother would die soon.

As if reading her mind, Mrs. Greene asked, "How is Mrs. Wittmer?"

"As well as can be expected. She's refusing any major medical intervention. She only agreed to drugs to control the seizures and the pain."

Mrs. Greene patted his cheek. "You'll be fine, my dear boy. You'll be fine. A handsome man like you will meet some nice young woman." She pressed her index finger to her mouth. "My friend Mildred has a granddaughter…"

Spencer waved her off and laughed. "Cut a guy a break."

"Cut yourself one, too."

"Night, Mrs. Greene."

Mrs. Greene held up a hang-on-a-minute finger. She pivoted in her slippers, her colorful housecoat a sight to see, and scooted into her apartment. She returned a minute later with a covered dish. "I figured you didn't have a chance to eat dinner. I made you my meat loaf."

He smiled. "I love your meat loaf."

"I know." She crossed her arms, a smug expression on her face.

That night, Hannah made sure her mother was comfortable with tea and her knitting next to her rocker. Her mother wasn't quite ready for bed and wanted to sit up for a bit.

Hannah, still dressed in her English clothes, planned to collect some of Ruthie's Amish clothes from the main house and while there, check on Emma and Sarah. Hannah hated to let the girls out of her sight, but it only made sense to allow them to sleep in their old house.

Hannah stepped outside, and the sound of crickets filled the night air. The rich smell of earth reached her nose. There was something very comforting, soothing, nostalgic about the country life. A comfort she had never found in the city.

Most of her life, Hannah felt like she had been caught between two worlds. Never quite fitting in either.

Out by the street, a police cruiser slowed down. She knew it wasn't Spencer's. He had told her he had the rest of the night off. She waved, and the officer flicked his headlights in acknowledgement.

Hope pushed out her anxiety. Maybe whoever was so determined to bother her would back off once he thought she had committed to returning to the Amish faith. Unless, of course, his motive was to have her gone. *Period.* She stifled a shiver.

Hannah raced up the few steps to her sister's home, now Fannie Mae and Lester's. She knocked, feeling a little foolish since this has been her home not long ago. Lester pulled open the door as if he had been waiting for her. His mouth compressed, and his eyes narrowed just a fraction.

"I need to get clothes." Hannah wanted to diffuse the situation before it got volatile.

He stepped away from the door and kept on walking. Hannah didn't see Fannie Mae, so she entered the house and went directly upstairs. In her sister's old room, Hannah grabbed a few dresses from the trunk where she had stored them. For half a minute, she considered changing into the dress, then realized that would be silly. It was almost time to get ready for bed. She didn't want to create more laundry for herself. She swiped at her jeans and decided she wouldn't risk hanging them out on the line. She couldn't afford to replace more clothes.

But you won't need your English clothes anymore.

She rubbed the back of her neck, praying God would guide her toward the right path.

Hannah hustled out of her sister's old bedroom, feeling like an interloper now that Lester and Fannie Mae were living there. Sleeping there. Across the hall she found Sarah reading to Emma. Hannah's heart expanded when she realized it was the *Little House on the Prairie* book she had given Sarah. She stood in the doorway for a few minutes, taking in the scene, not wanting to disturb them. They both had long pajama dresses on, reminiscent of those she had seen the actress Melissa Gilbert wearing in the old TV show adapted from the books.

The thought that she'd have to show the girls that program left as quickly as it came. Sarah and Emma wouldn't be watching TV anytime soon, if ever.

Was that such a bad thing?

Emma was the first to notice her aunt standing in the doorway. She scooted off the bed and ran over to Hannah and wrapped her arms around her aunt's waist. "Are you going to stay here?"

Hannah placed the clothes down on the chair near the door. Tears pricked the back of her eyes. She flicked her thumb toward the *dawdy haus.* "I'll stay with Granny."

"I'm glad she's not sick anymore." Clearly, Emma assumed her grandmother's homecoming meant she was all better. She gave Emma a little squeeze. Sarah looked up from her book for the first time.

"Everything okay?" Hannah asked.

Sarah shrugged.

Hannah guided Emma over to the bed. Hannah sat next to Sarah and pulled Emma onto her lap. "Are you not happy here?"

Sarah scratched her hair, where her bun met the back of her neck. "I liked school."

"You can go to school."

Sarah shyly shook her head. "I liked my new school."

Hannah's heart thundered in her ears. She suddenly felt guilty. Poor Sarah and Emma were unwitting pawns in her indecisive life.

Hannah cleared her throat. "Right now, you can't go to Apple Creek Elementary." She bit her bottom lip, wondering if there was any way she could make arrangements. It was impossible, given the circumstances.

Sarah slumped into her pillow. "Mrs. Gallivan said I'm good at math."

"I have an idea. Why don't I talk to your old teacher and get the assignments and we can work at home together."

"Really?"

"Really."

Sarah's entire face transformed from glum to hopeful with one little word.

"I like math, too," Emma said, resting her head on Hannah's shoulder.

"I can help you with math, too."

"Girls, I think it's time for bed." Lester appeared in the doorway, looking stern. Hannah almost jumped out of her skin. How long had he been standing there?

"Did you brush your teeth?" Hannah forced a smile, trying to ease the nerves clawing at her throat.

Both girls nodded.

"Then I guess you're ready for bed." Hannah took the book from Sarah's lap and set it on the nightstand. She stood, and Emma climbed into the warm spot next to her sister. "Night girls. See you in the morning."

"Night, Aunt Hannah," they said in unison, using the English word *aunt* and not *aenti* as they had when she first arrived.

Hannah gave them one last tuck and a kiss on the forehead. She scooped the dresses up from the chair and brushed past Lester, whose anger was rolling off him in waves.

Smiling smugly, as if she had won a small battle today, Hannah descended the steps. As she was coming down, Fannie Mae hustled up. "Are you ready for bed, girls?"

Hannah stopped on the steps. "They're all set."

Fannie Mae gave her a sidelong glance and kept climbing the stairs. Hannah reached the door and stepped outside onto the porch. The cool air felt good on her fiery cheeks. Gloating from her one small win had been fleeting.

Hannah drew in and released several deep breaths, hoping to calm her emotions. She felt like she was losing everything that was important to her. The door opened behind her. Hannah swiped away at her tears and squared her shoulders. The heavy footsteps told her it was Lester. Her heart dropped. He approached and eyed her English clothes and the bundle of Amish clothing in her arms.

He took off his straw hat and rubbed his head. "Fannie Mae and I would love those girls as our own."

"I...I..." Hannah's mouth went dry, and she couldn't form the words.

"My father believes your mother's illness has brought you back again. To fully commit to the Amish way." He leaned in close. He smelled of hay and horse and apple butter. "*Yah*, well, I don't think that's your plan."

Their gazes locked. She made a conscious decision not to lie to him.

She had done enough lying to herself.

Hannah rolled over for what seemed to be the hundredth time on the tiny cot she had set up in the sitting room of her mother's small home. She tugged on the quilt and covered her shoulder, unable to get comfortable. She held her breath and listened intently for any sign her mother was in distress. She resisted the urge to get up and go into her room. Last time she had, her mother said, "I'm not dead. Yet." The droll tone was very uncharacteristic of her mother.

The physician had rattled off all the potential effects of a growing tumor as it pressed on the brain.

Hannah suspected she was trying to frighten her mother into agreeing to treatment. But you can't frighten a woman who has her faith, and a woman who is more afraid of the treatment than the effects of not treating it.

Resigned that sleep wasn't coming anytime soon, Hannah swung her feet over the edge of the cot and sat up. The cool evening air touched her skin, sending a chill skittering down her spine. Wrapping the quilt around her shoulders, she stood. As if lured by worry, she found herself lurking in her mother's doorway. Her mother rolled over and tugged at her sheet.

Regret for all the years she had been estranged from her family weighted heavily on her. All the years she had missed.

A creak on the front porch made her breath hitch in her throat.

Creak.

Hot tingles swept across her scalp. Clutching the quilt closer to her shoulders, she moved silently through the small home. She slid open the drawer in the hutch and pulled out her cell phone. The reality of how vulnerable she was out here on the farm struck her. Even if she dialed Spencer's number, how fast could he get here?

She heard a quiet knock and a voice, "Aunt Hannah?"

Hannah dropped the phone on the doily her

grandmother had made and ran to the door. She undid the bolt and flung the door open.

"Sarah?" Confusion swirled in her head. Deep in the house, she heard her mother cough then grow quiet. Hannah stepped out onto the porch and pulled the door over, leaving it ajar so she could hear her mother.

"It's late. What are you doing here?"

Sarah lifted and dropped her shoulders. Perhaps she had lost her nerve for whatever had brought her out into the night.

Hannah guided Sarah to the steps and they sat. Staring into the dark yard, Hannah waited. Out by the street, a lamppost lit a small sphere of country road. Finally, Sarah shifted to face her. "I'm sorry for being grumpy."

Hannah smiled. She remembered her mother using that expression anytime Hannah or her sister Ruthie was in a bad mood. It was such a pleasant way of saying they had been downright intolerable. Ruthie must have repeated the expression to her daughters.

Hannah took a chance and reached out and wrapped her arm around her niece's shoulder. Sarah leaned her head on Hannah's shoulder, and Hannah's heart expanded. "You've lost a lot, sweetie. You don't have to apologize to me."

Sarah looked up. Tears glistened under the moonlight. "I don't want to lose you, Aunt Hannah."

"Oh, sweetie, you're not going to lose me."

"*Mem* always told me what a great sister you were. She told me and Emma we needed to always look out for each other."

A band tightened around Hannah's lungs making it hard to catch a breath. Had she been there for her sister?

"I wasn't always the best big sister. I wish I could have been there for your *mem* when she really needed me."

Sarah swiped at a tear. "*Mem* always spoke fondly of you."

"You seem wise for a little girl."

"I'm not so little."

"You're young enough that you shouldn't have had to deal with so many adult problems."

"I promise I'll be nicer to Emma."

Hannah swatted at a mosquito. "Are your worries keeping you awake?"

Sarah's voice got very tiny. "I thought if I was nice to you it meant finally accepting that *Mem* was…" She bowed her head and her shoulders shook.

Hannah pulled her closer. "I'll never replace your *mem*. No one can. But I'll try to be the best aunt ever."

Sarah sucked in a shaky breath. "When you leave, I want to go with you."

Hannah pulled back to look into Sarah's eyes. "Why do you think I'm going to leave?"

"I heard Uncle Lester talking to Aunt Fannie

Mae. He said that Emma and me would be staying with them."

Hot anger pulsed through Hannah's veins. Footsteps crunched on the dried bent grass. Pinpricks of apprehension coursed across Hannah's skin. She reached up and grabbed the handrail, rising to her feet even as her knees felt weak. She scanned the yard.

Maybe it was an animal.

Hannah was about to urge Sarah to go inside, when a deep voice boomed from the shadows.

"What are you doing out of bed, Sarah?"

The anger in Lester's voice vibrated through Hannah. It slammed her back to another time. Her father's harsh reprimand. Followed by his firm hand. Hannah squared her shoulders. "Sarah was feeling unsettled—"

"Of course she feels unsettled. You've pulled her away from the only home she's ever known. She should have stayed here. Where she belongs."

Sweat slicked her palms. Suddenly, she felt very exposed. Alone. Defenseless.

Her phone was inside the house on the hutch.

Hannah leaned down and whispered into Sarah's ear, "Go inside. Lock the door. My cell phone is on the table. Call Spencer."

The word *why* formed on Sarah's lips when Lester exploded. "Stop corrupting the child."

Sarah got to her feet and sprinted inside, but the

door yawned open. She willed the child to close and lock it.

Hannah's raspy breaths sounded in her ears.

She moved behind the railing on the porch, and thankfully, Lester didn't advance on her.

He lifted his beefy hand and pointed at the door. "Sarah needs to come home with me where she belongs."

Hannah shook her head. "She belongs with me."

A second man emerged from the shadows. Hannah froze, wide-eyed. The man's arms came around fast and furious. He brought a board down on Lester's head before Hannah could get a scream across her dry lips.

Lester went down in a silent heap, not knowing what hit him.

"She belongs among us." Willard Fisher's angry snarl registered under the moonlight. Fear rained down on her, hot and tingly. Hannah spun around to get inside. Lock the door.

Willard dove, and his hand wrapped around her ankles and she landed with an *oomph* on the porch, the air rushing out of her lungs. She opened her mouth to warn Sarah, to tell her to close the door, lock the door, but she couldn't catch a breath.

Willard yanked her by the ankles. Her body thumped down the stairs. Her ribs. Her elbow. Her hip.

Hannah violently shook and twisted her body, trying to free her ankles from Willard's brutal grasp. She thought she heard a mischievous laugh as he dragged her around the side of the house into the darkness.

SIXTEEN

Spencer pulled into the Lapps' dirt driveway, his headlights arcing across the darkened home. The memory of Sarah's frantic sobs over the phone rang in his ears. *Hannah's in trouble.* A trail of sweat ran between his shoulder blades. He pushed open his door and aimed the flashlight around the yard. The beam of light hit on a prone form.

For an instant, his heart stuttered, then his brain kicked in. It wasn't Hannah. It was a man, an Amish man. Walking toward the body, he swept the flashlight around the yard.

No one else in sight.

Aware of his surroundings, he crouched. Lester Lapp lay unconscious with his nose mashed into the dirt. Spencer pressed his fingers to Lester's neck. His pulse was steady.

Had Hannah knocked out Lester? His pulse ticked up a notch. What if she hadn't?

He strained to listen for sounds of distress. Nothing but crickets.

The headlights from his vehicle stretched to the front porch. The front door was open, and a little girl stepped out. He had to squint to realize it was Sarah.

"Stay on the porch." He held up his hand and scanned the area. The adrenaline surge heightened all his senses. The scene was different, but the feelings were the same. Little Daniel had died under his watch. Someone had called dispatch from the convenience store. Gangs had gathered in front of the store. By the time he got there, Daniel was dead. An innocent victim.

Spencer blinked back his mounting anxiety. He wasn't going to let anyone else die.

Spencer moved to the porch and ushered Sarah inside and locked the door behind them. He canvassed the small space. Empty save for Mrs. Wittmer sleeping in her bed.

Back in the sitting area, he crouched in front of Sarah. "Where's Hannah?"

Every inch of her small frame trembled.

"You're safe now. Tell me what happened."

Sarah relayed a story about missing Hannah and then her uncle yelling at her and Hannah got afraid and told her to call him.

That didn't explain Lester unconscious on the lawn. "Did Hannah and Lester fight?"

Spencer's nerves hummed as he pried answers out of the frightened girl.

"I heard angry voices. I didn't see. I hid inside.

I'm sorry." Sarah buried her face in her hands and sobbed.

Spencer nodded, trying to maintain his composure. "I'm going to find Hannah. I want you to lock this door behind me. Do you know how to do that?"

Sarah shook her head. Spencer took pains to show Sarah how to work the lock. He stepped onto the porch and listened to Sarah fasten the lock. He tested the door.

"Stay inside until I come get you. Don't open this door for anyone except me."

Sarah didn't answer, but he was sure she heard him through the thin door. A thin door that wouldn't hold back anyone determined to get in. But he feared the person who had been here already had the person he wanted.

Spencer cast the beam of the flashlight around the yard, and that's when he saw it: a pink bandanna had been discarded at the corner of the house. Heart beating loudly in his ears, he strode toward the bandanna. Hannah had had one in her hair earlier.

When he reached the corner of the house, he saw nothing but grass stretching toward the neighbor's cornfields. His heart sank.

Hannah could be anywhere.

"If you scream, I'll make it worse. I'll go back into that house and make that disobedient child remember the rules," Willard growled as he lumbered across the yard, dragging Hannah by one ankle.

Hannah bit back a gasp. Willard's strong fingers dug into her flesh. The more she fought and thrashed about, the more pain shot up her legs and thighs.

Panic and fear clouded her brain. Her back and arms bounced off the uneven earth. Her body flipped and she braced her fists against the earth to protect her head, her face.

Dear Lord, help me. Help me...

Tears burned the backs of her eyes, and she drew in a deep breath. Willard dragged her into the cornfields. Stalks whacked her arms, and she squeezed her eyes shut against the assault.

No one will find me out here. Please Lord, spare me. Don't take me away from Sarah and Emma. Please...

Willard stopped and in one quick swoop, pressed his knee into her back, crushing the air from her lungs. He leaned in close and whispered in her ear, "You couldn't just leave. *Neh*, you had to force your worldly ways on all of us. You are no better than your sister."

Hannah briefly closed her eyes and fought the wave of grief that washed over her. She focused instead on the pain radiating out from where his knee pressed into her spine, channeling it into survival mode.

Willard forced her cheek into the earth. The

smell of dried corn and manure plugged her nose. She bit back nausea.

"John couldn't control her. Ruth needed to be obedient to him."

Hannah strained to watch Willard out of the corner of her eye. He was watching something, searching. Was someone coming?

"So you killed them? You killed Ruthie…and John?"

Willard pushed her head deeper into the damp earth. Something in her neck cracked. "I did what was necessary to preserve the Amish way. I've lived in the outside world. It's an evil place. The Amish must be ruthless in preserving their quality of life. They must be separate. John had been on my side, but when Ruthie started questioning him, John was weak. He softened his stance. I couldn't allow her to destroy our plans. To destroy the Amish way of life."

Willard's weight and her panic pressed on her chest. "Is murder the Amish way?"

"Shut up."

"You wrote the note making it look like John had committed suicide?" She spit out a chunk of dirt.

"*Yah.* Yet you still wouldn't leave. I thought once you knew John wasn't coming back, you'd hand the children over to a good Amish home." Willard roughly dragged his fingers through her short hair. "A woman's hair is her glory. You…" He seemed to lose his train of thought, pushing harder on her back. Hannah sucked in shallow breaths as tiny stars danced in her line of vision.

"You corrupted my son. You corrupted your nieces. Your death is one small sacrifice to make things right."

"No...no." Hannah's brain whirled, but she couldn't form the words, the words to plead for her life.

"But Lester..." She couldn't think straight.

"Lester never saw what hit him. Even he couldn't make his brother see the light." He laughed, a mirthless sound. "The brothers came to blows in town when John got the foolish idea to leave the farm for other work. What fools."

"The sheriff—"

"The sheriff's office is incompetent. It took them ten years to solve Mary Miller's disappearance, remember that?"

The delight in his words made her blood run cold. "Don't underestimate Sheriff Maxwell. He'll find you."

Willard leaned in close. "Some things are worth the sacrifice." Stale breath washed over her and made her gag.

Willard shifted his weight, and Hannah rolled, just far enough to fall out of the cornfield and onto the open field. She filled her lungs with fresh air.

Willard lunged for her, his features contorted in anger. She rolled again and scrambled to her feet.

He grabbed her by her hair and yanked. "You're not getting away."

"No!" The word ripped from her throat.

The beam of Spencer's flashlight landed on Hannah as she furiously tried to wiggle free from Willard Fisher's grasp.

Tightening his hold on his gun, Spencer bolted across the yard. Willard spun Hannah around and wrapped an arm around her neck. "Easy, *Englischer.*"

Spencer leveled his gun at Willard's head. "Let her go." Spencer bit out the words, his breath coming in jagged rasps.

"You wouldn't shoot an Amish man, would you? Think of all your hard work to mend bridges between law enforcement and the Amish."

Hannah yanked on Willard's arm stretched across her chest. Willard flipped out a pocketknife and pressed it against her neck.

"Drop it."

"I'll stick her like a pig." Willard's gleeful expression twisted Spencer's gut. His finger twitched on the trigger.

"Dat, neh!" Samuel ran up to Spencer. "Stop!"

"Get back, son," Spencer said, not taking his eyes from Willard.

Samuel stood his ground. "No. Stop."

The lines around Willard's lips grew pinched, agitated. "Go home."

"No. I will not let you hurt Hannah. She's done nothing wrong."

"Her ways are poison. Poison to the Amish ways. Poison to *you*."

Samuel shook his head, a maturity about him Spencer had never noticed before. "You have become poison."

Willard's face twitched, a mix of grief and rage. His hand loosened around the knife. Spencer took the opening and slammed Willard's shoulder, knocking him away from Hannah. The knife flew from his grip and landed in the field.

Spencer pushed Willard facedown into the earth and handcuffed him. Spencer dragged him to his feet. Willard rearranged his features into one of smugness.

Hannah stood apart from them, rubbing her neck. Spencer wanted to do nothing more than take her into his arms. Thank God she was safe. But for now, he had to take Willard in to the station.

"He killed Ruth and John." Hannah's tone was one of anger and grief.

"No one will believe you." Willard narrowed his gaze.

"He made me destroy your clothes on the line," Samuel said, pacing pack and forth. "He made me give Emma and Sarah the cat." He drew in a ragged breath and glared at his father. "He *made me* tell them bad things would happen to their kitty if they said anything—" his voice grew quiet "—but he…

he burned down the barn. He wanted to punish me for reading in the loft. To punish you, Miss Wittmer. I don't know what else he's done. But he's been obsessed with running you out of town, and he tried to force me to help him. He made me lie and tell you I saw John Lapp out by the barn before it went up in flames." Samuel bowed his head briefly. "After I ruined your clothes, the guilt was terrible." The young man sniffed, and his shoulders shook.

"Shut up," Willard spat out. "You're a fence jumper, just like the worthless rest of them."

"Like you, *Dat*. You left…" Samuel's stern tone belied his trembling lips. "I wish you never came back."

A siren grew closer. Spencer pushed Willard in handcuffs toward the driveway. Willard's chest heaved from unspent anger.

Hannah brushed her hand across Spencer's forearm. "I'll go check on Sarah and my mom." Spencer nodded.

Deputy Sheriff Mark Reynolds's cruiser bounced up the driveway. Spencer squinted against the glare of the headlights. Mark climbed out, a smirk on his lips. "Looks like you got this one all wrapped up yourself."

Spencer handed off Willard. "Take care of him. And make sure Lester Lapp receives medical attention."

"Stupid fool got in my way. He can't have much

more than a big lump and a headache." Willard shook his head, a look of disgust on his face. "I couldn't let Lester see what I was about to do. Wrong place, wrong time."

"Thanks," Spencer said wryly. "We can add additional assault charges to the long list. Take him," he said to the officer. "I've got something else to handle."

Mark pushed Willard roughly toward the cruiser. "Wait," Spencer called out. "How did you get the note in Emma's backpack?"

Willard narrowed his gaze. "Don't you want to know if I chopped off her hair first?"

"No, I know you did that because you put the lock of hair with the note in Emma's bag." Spencer studied the man's face in the moonlight. Willard seemed more angry than anything else.

"It wasn't hard to grab her backpack after she tossed it down when she ran off to the playground. It took two seconds to stuff the envelope in her bag then drop it behind a tree as I strolled away. No one seemed to notice me. Even if they had, they'd only remember seeing an Amish man, not me specifically." Willard blinked slowly.

Spencer gestured with his chin toward the car. "Now you can take him away." Spencer watched as Mark stuffed Willard into the backseat of the cruiser. All the tough guy seemed to have drained out of him.

Spencer turned around and cupped Samuel's shoulder. "You did well, kid."

Hannah came back outside and made her way across the lawn holding Sarah's hand. "My mother's still sleeping," she said. "The EMT is tending to Lester. He's conscious, but he's got a wallop of a headache. He's refusing to go to the hospital."

"I'll make sure he goes," Spencer said.

Hannah nodded.

Samuel's features grew pinched, a faraway look in his eyes. "I hate my *dat*. I hate everything he represents." He lifted his gaze to Hannah. "I'm sorry." He held out his hand to Sarah. The young girl leaned her head against Hannah's side. "I'm sorry I scared you. I would never hurt you or your cat."

"It's okay," Sarah said in a soft voice. "I never saw anyone do anything bad. I never had to keep a secret."

"Eventually, you will have to find a way to forgive yourself. To forgive your father. To free yourself from the burden." Hannah's tone was full of understanding.

Samuel nodded, clearly not convinced.

"I can drive you home, Samuel," Spencer offered. "Your statement can wait until tomorrow.

"I need to clear my head. I'll walk home."

"I'd feel better if I drove you."

Samuel shook his head. "The evil is gone. I'll be fine."

Spencer and Hannah stood in silence as Samuel walked across the field, his shoulders slumped with a burden no son should carry.

Sarah looked up. "May I go inside with Granny?"

"Of course." Hannah kissed her niece's forehead, and they watched her run into the house.

Spencer pulled Hannah into an embrace. "I don't ever want to lose you again." She pulled back and looked up at him; something flashed across her eyes. A band around his heart squeezed. "I suppose we'll have to figure out this Amish thing."

Hannah laughed, a beautiful sound. "I don't suppose you'll be converting anytime soon." She patted his cheek and laughed even louder. "Oh, you should see the look on your face." She rested her forehead against his shoulder.

"I love you, Hannah Wittmer."

He held his breath as the silence stretched between them.

Finally, finally, Hannah lifted her head. A slow smile spread across her face. "I love you, too."

EPILOGUE

Four months later...

Hannah wrapped the scarf around her neck and hustled down the porch steps to wait for the school bus. Winter had hunkered down for the long haul in sleepy little Apple Creek, New York.

The squealing of the bus brakes signaled its approach before she saw its big yellow body rounding the corner. She waved at the bus driver, indicating the new stop. It was the girls' first day back at the public school.

The bus doors slid open with a whoosh, and Emma appeared in the doorway, looking happy and cute as pie in her matching Hello Kitty hat, scarf and gloves. She hopped off the bus and Hannah planted a kiss on her niece's cool cheek.

"How was your first day back?"

"My teacher told me I knew just as much as the other kids." Emma dropped her backpack on the snowy walkway, and Hannah picked it up. "You did a good job teaching us at home."

Hannah's heart expanded at Emma's cheery report. She shifted her gaze toward the bus. Sarah was chatting animatedly to a girl in the front seat. Then she bounded down the stairs. "I met a friend who lives down the street. Do you think we can have a playdate?"

Tears burned the back of Hannah's eyes. Happy tears. "Of course." She didn't bother asking her older niece if she had a good day. It was abundantly clear that she had.

A gust of snow whipped up and drifted under Hannah's collar. "Let's get inside. I'll make us some hot chocolate."

The girls ran ahead and greeted Mrs. Greene in the foyer as they passed.

"Take your boots off," Hannah hollered up the stairs as she closed the door behind her.

Mrs. Greene held out a plate. "Here are some chocolate chip cookies to go with that hot chocolate."

"You're spoiling us," Hannah said, gratitude filling her heart.

"I can't take credit. Your friend Rebecca dropped them off."

Hannah tugged at her scarf. "Rebecca?" Hannah hadn't spoken with her friend since the day after her husband, Willard, was arrested. Back then,

Rebecca had been hurt and angry and had turned her childhood friend away.

"Your friend has such beautiful skin." Mrs. Greene lifted her hand to her wrinkled cheek and then seemed to mentally shake herself. "She said she was sorry and she hoped to see you soon. She seems like such a dear girl."

Hannah drew in a deep breath and smiled. "That's very good news. I'll have to take a drive to visit her." Through the Apple Creek grapevine, she had heard Rebecca was fairing surprisingly well. Perhaps she found peace in being out from under Willard's oppressive thumb now that he was in jail, most likely for the rest of his life.

Mrs. Greene looked at Hannah thoughtfully. "I'm *so* happy to have you back. The girls fill my quiet home with laughter. It's a blessing." Mrs. Greene fidgeted with the edge of her apron. "I'm sorry I wasn't able to do more for you and your mother when she was ill."

"My mother and I had plenty of support from her Amish friends." Hannah smiled at the bittersweet memory of her mother's last days. Although the brain tumor had zapped her strength, it hadn't diminished her faith. And mother and daughter had grown especially close in those last few months.

Hannah hesitated a minute then glanced up the stairs. "Would you like to join us for our afternoon snack?"

"Oh, no." Mrs. Greene waved in dismissal. "You're busy."

A stomping sounded on the porch. Through the sheers on the door, she saw Spencer in his sheriff's uniform. She pulled open the door, a wide smile on her face. "Fancy meeting you here."

He kissed her on the forehead with cold lips, warming her heart. "I wanted to see how the girls made out their first day back at school."

"Great! Come on up, I promised them hot chocolate." Hannah turned to go upstairs while Spencer closed the door behind him. "Can I talk to you first?"

Mrs. Greene's eyebrows shot up. "Why don't I keep the girls company while you chat?"

Hannah smiled, pleased Mrs. Greene had gotten over her reluctance to join them. "That would be wonderful." Hannah handed over the chocolate chip cookies.

After Mrs. Greene went into Hannah's apartment, Hannah turned to Spencer. "It's really snowy out there."

He tipped his head and gave her a look, a look that said, *We're not going to talk about the weather, are we?*

"How are you doing?" The sincerity in Spencer's voice warmed her heart.

"Better. I miss my mom, but I know she's in a better place."

Spencer nodded. He reached out and held her hand. "She was blessed to have you."

"And I was blessed to have her." She bowed her head; a tear fell unbidden down her cheek.

He dragged his knuckles tenderly across her cheek. "I hope your mother didn't mind my visits. I did the best to respect the Amish ways."

"My mom really liked you. I'm glad she got to know you." She leaned into his hand.

"What's not to like?" A light twinkled in his eyes.

"We never spoke of it, but my mother and I came to an understanding. She's at peace with my decision to leave the Amish. She knows my faith is strong. She knows I'll do what's best for the girls."

"I'm happy for you." He paused long enough for her to wonder what was on his mind. "I have good news."

Hannah's heart raced. She swallowed hard. "About the girls?"

"Yes." Half his mouth quirked into a grin. "I ran into that lawyer Jones in town. He told me the Lapps weren't going to fight for custody of Emma and Sarah."

"Really?" she said on a huge breath of relief.

"That's what he said. I'm sure you'll have to sign a few legal forms. The lawyer seemed surprised the Amish don't like to deal with the court system. I suppose if Jones knew that, he would have never approached them in the first place."

"I'm sure that was part of it," Hannah said, brushing a dusting of snow from Spencer's shoulder, "but I also want to believe the Lapps came to realize over the past few months how much I love the girls. And that they're happy with me."

"I'm happy with you." The intensity in his gaze tangled nerves in her belly. "You have brought so much into my life. I finally feel I have found my purpose. God's purpose for my life. I can't thank you enough."

Hannah drew in a shaky breath and watched him through blurry eyes. "Thank *you* for being patient with me."

"You're worth the wait." Spencer leaned in and pressed his lips to hers. He deepened the kiss, sending tingles of awareness coursing through her body.

"Are you going to be my new dad?" Emma appeared at the top of the stairs. She had already dropped the Amish *dat* for dad.

Hannah and Spencer pulled away. Embarrassment added to the heat of the kiss.

Sarah appeared and put her hands on her little sister's shoulders. "*Are* you going to be our new dad?"

Kids adjust easily, her mother had said during the final days of her life. Her mother had given her lots of pearls of wisdom that kept popping into her head now that she was gone.

"Girls!" Hannah playfully scolded.

"Would you like that?" Spencer asked the girls and squeezed Hannah's hand.

They both nodded eagerly.

Hannah turned to look at Spencer. Hesitation flashed across his features, and for one horrifying moment, Hannah thought Spencer looked like a deer caught in the headlights. A slow smile transformed his face. He unzipped his coat and reached into his inside coat pocket. Her pulse thrummed in her ears.

Spencer pulled out a small black box, and Hannah almost passed out with surprise. Her vision tunneled onto his handsome face.

He dropped to one knee right there on the slushy-wet foyer carpet. He popped open the box, revealing a solitaire diamond engagement ring.

"Will you marry me, Hannah Wittmer?"

Lifting her free hand to her mouth, she nodded. Tears flooded her eyes.

"What did she say?" Mrs. Greene asked from the top landing.

Hannah and Spencer laughed in unison.

"Yes," Hannah said while he pulled himself to his feet. "Yes, yes, yes…I'll marry you."

Spencer slipped the ring onto her finger and lifted her hand to his lips. "I love you."

The thudding of little feet racing down the stairs broke the trance. Hannah and Spencer held out their arms and pulled the girls into their embrace.

"Well, if this ain't better than the afternoon soaps, I don't know what is." Mrs. Greene held up a finger. "I hear the kettle. Time to celebrate with some hot chocolate."

Spencer and Hannah climbed the stairs to her upstairs apartment, his arm wrapped around her. The little girls ran ahead.

"I never thought I could be this happy," Hannah said, thinking about all the failed attempts to fit in throughout her life.

"I know what you mean."

When they entered her apartment, Hannah stopped and turned to face him. "Where will we live once we get married? Your apartment or mine?"

Without a moment's hesitation, as if he had been considering this a long time already, he said, "I had my eye on a little hobby farm in Apple Creek. If you want, we can take a drive out tomorrow to look at it."

Excitement bubbled in her chest. "You've given this some thought."

"Yes, and I've also given something else some thought."

Hannah jerked back her head, confused.

Spencer dramatically placed an index finger on

his lips. "I bet two little girls would like a kitty for our new home."

Emma's eyes grew wide. "Yes!" She hugged him around the waist.

Spencer placed his hand on Emma's back. "I talked to Rebecca yesterday. She told me Pumpkin would be much happier with you and Sarah."

Sarah dropped the cookie she had picked up and ran over and hugged both Emma and Spencer. Hannah's heart melted all over again.

"Thank you," Hannah mouthed to her future husband.

A warm smile played on his lips.

Hannah approached her little family and placed her arm around her future husband.

"Now, who am I going to fuss over if you four move out?" Mrs. Greene's lips twisted into an I-don't-know-what-I'll-do smirk.

"Why do we think you'll be just fine?" Spencer winked at the older woman who had become like a grandmother to him. "Besides, we're not moving far."

Mrs. Greene blushed and a mischievous grin lit her face. "You got a good one here, Hannah. Good thing I'm not a few years younger." She hustled to the stove and lifted the kettle from the burner. "Who wants whipped cream in their hot chocolate?"

Emma and Sarah ran over to the island and sat down. Spencer wrapped his arm around Hannah's shoulders. A feeling of contentedness settled over her like a warm shawl on a snowy afternoon. She turned and whispered to Spencer, "I finally feel like I belong."

"Me, too," Spencer said. "Me, too."

* * * * *

*Look for more gripping stories
from Alison Stone later in 2015.
You'll find them wherever
Love Inspired Suspense Books are sold!*

Dear Reader,

I hoped you enjoyed *Plain Peril*. It's my second Harlequin Love Inspired Suspense set in Apple Creek, NY. The first was *Plain Pursuit*. The fictional Apple Creek is loosely based on the real Amish community along Route 62 in Conewango Valley, NY, about an hour drive from Buffalo, NY. It wasn't until I started research for my first Amish book, that I realized an Amish community existed so close to my hometown. Imagine my surprise!

Everything Amish seems to be popular these days, and fiction is no exception. Writing suspense around the constraints of Amish characters is both fun and challenging. Challenging because my editor will make a note on the manuscript such as, "Where is she charging her cell phone?" (My heroine is reluctant to leave behind her English ways.) Finding creative ways to work around these problems is part of the fun.

In real life, the Amish are very creative, too. On one visit to Conewango Valley, my daughters and I stopped at an Amish candy shop. They were able to use a modern mixer by threading the electrical cord through an opening to the outside where they had it connected to a gas-powered generator. Ta-da! Electricity! In many Amish communities, electricity is acceptable as long as the house is not connected to the grid.

I've enjoyed learning and writing about the Amish. I look forward to future visits to Apple Creek.

I love to hear from my readers. Feel free to send me a note at my email address: *Alison@AlisonStone.com*. Or "like" me on Facebook: https://www.facebook.com/AlisonStoneAuthor.

Alison Stone

LARGER-PRINT BOOKS!

GET 2 FREE
LARGER-PRINT NOVELS
PLUS 2 FREE
MYSTERY GIFTS

Love Inspired®

Larger-print novels are now available...

LILPDIR13R

REQUEST YOUR FREE BOOKS!
2 FREE WHOLESOME ROMANCE NOVELS IN LARGER PRINT
PLUS 2 FREE MYSTERY GIFTS

✶✶✶✶✶✶✶✶✶✶✶✶✶✶✶✶✶✶✶✶✶✶

H E A R T W A R M I N G™

✶✶✶✶✶✶✶✶✶✶✶✶✶✶✶✶✶✶✶✶✶✶✶✶

Wholesome, tender romances

YES! Please send me 2 FREE Harlequin® Heartwarming Larger-Print novels and my 2 FREE mystery gifts (gifts worth about $10). After receiving them, if I don't wish to receive any more books, I can return the shipping statement marked "cancel." If I don't cancel, I will receive 4 brand-new larger-print novels every month and be billed just $4.99 per book in the U.S. or $5.74 per book in Canada. That's a savings of at least 23% off the cover price. It's quite a bargain! Shipping and handling is just 50¢ per book in the U.S. and 75¢ per book in Canada.* I understand that accepting the 2 free books and gifts places me under no obligation to buy anything. I can always return a shipment and cancel at any time. Even if I never buy another book, the two free books and gifts are mine to keep forever.

161/361 IDN F47N

Name _____ (PLEASE PRINT)

Address _____ Apt. #

City _____ State/Prov. _____ Zip/Postal Code

Signature (if under 18, a parent or guardian must sign)

Mail to the **Harlequin® Reader Service:**
IN U.S.A.: P.O. Box 1867, Buffalo, NY 14240-1867
IN CANADA: P.O. Box 609, Fort Erie, Ontario L2A 5X3

* Terms and prices subject to change without notice. Prices do not include applicable taxes. Sales tax applicable in N.Y. Canadian residents will be charged applicable taxes. Offer not valid in Quebec. This offer is limited to one order per household. Not valid for current subscribers to Harlequin Heartwarming larger-print books. All orders subject to credit approval. Credit or debit balances in a customer's account(s) may be offset by any other outstanding balance owed by or to the customer. Please allow 4 to 6 weeks for delivery. Offer available while quantities last.

HWDIR13R

ReaderService.com

Manage your account online!

- Review your order history
- Manage your payments
- Update your address

*We've designed
the Harlequin® Reader Service
website just for you.*

Enjoy all the features!

- Reader excerpts from any series
- Respond to mailings and
  special monthly offers
- Discover new series available to you
- Browse the Bonus Bucks catalog
- Share your feedback

Visit us at:

ReaderService.com